Amy's Story

A Novel

Amy's Story

A Novel

by Anna Lawton

THE SPRING

Washington, DC

Printed in the United States of America

Library of Congress Control Number: 2016915448
ISBN 978-0-9974962-1-5 paperback (alk. paper)
ISBN 978-0-9974962-0-8 hardcover (alk. paper)

THE SPRING   **The Spring** is an imprint of New Academia Publishing

New Academia Publishing
4401-A Connecticut Ave. NW #236, Washington DC 20008
info@newacademia.com - www.newacademia.com

Memory moves constantly. It's not like going to the storage room and picking up a thing that has been sitting there unchanged. We have already been working for years on that thing.

— *Umberto Eco*

(La memoria è sempre in movimento. Non è qualcosa che ci permette di andare in magazzino e prendere una cosa come era là senza che nessuno l'abbia modificata. È già una cosa su cui noi abbiamo lavorato durante gli anni.)

Contents

PART ONE

Beginning from the End (2001)

I

New York, September 2001

"Mulberry and Canal, please."

The cabbie looks at her in the rearview mirror while the car pulls off into the Broadway traffic.

"Are you a tourist?"

"No, I'm a New Yorker."

"But you were not born in New York?"

This puts her off. This really puts her off. Thirty plus years in this country and they still pick up traces of her Italian accent. Traces, mind you. It's practically all gone.

"Were *you*?" she asks, staring at the prayer beads dangling from the mirror. There is a note of irritation in her voice. The mirror sends back to her the liquid gaze of two dark eyes, now slightly sweetened with the hint of a smile.

"None of my business, miss. Just trying to make conversation."

Okay, he wants to be friendly. Let's be friendly.

"So, where are *you* from?"

"Afghanistan."

Image association. Amy sees flashes of Soviet tanks roaming the country, ambushes on mountain passes, destroyed cities and villages—the footage she used to see in the news twenty years ago. Then, she recalls recent humanitarian appeals for women executed in sport fields, their *burkas* looking like the hoods of witches burnt at the stake in medieval times.

"How long've you been here?" she asks.

"Since 1981. I was a kid. My family was among the lucky ones who made it. We loved our country, it was very beautiful. But then the Russians came, you know, they upset everything. And now a pack of mad dogs took power."

"Yeah, the Talibans. Is this what they're called? They're the ones who blew up those ancient Buddha sculptures, right?"

"I told you, miss, they're mad dogs. They say they rule according to sharia law. But this is not the Islam I know."

The cell rings. He picks up and starts an animated conversation. The cab fills up with harsh guttural sounds. He turns to her.

"Sorry, it's my wife. She wants me to take the kid to school today."

The conversation turns into an argument that does not seem to be going to end any time soon. Amy closes her eyes and dozes off, lulled by the traffic that rushes the car along like water in a stream.

It's a bright September morning. A quarter to eight, according to her watch. Amy hates going out that early, but this is the only time when she can have a quiet conversation with Rosa. At any other time, Rosa would be too busy with work at the pizzeria, all day long 'till late at night.

Rosa... Amy has known her for ages, since way back in Italy when she was a child and Rosa was a maid at Villa Flora, her grandmother's country estate. Here in New York they don't see each other often, only occasionally, when Amy feels like being pampered with a home-cooked meal and an outpouring of affection. But today she has to talk to Rosa about a matter related to work. She needs to verify a detail from the old times. It's for this manuscript she's getting ready for publication. A very special manuscript. The work of a childhood friend.

As the president of L&N Publishers, Amy does not do a lot of editing herself, not anymore. She has a dozen editors working for her. But this manuscript is really special. She would not entrust anyone with the job. It has to be her, because she's been so close to the author. They grew up together, they played together, they went to school together, and they spent the summer months together at Villa Flora. Amy and Stella, two inseparable friends. They even looked alike, although they had different personalities. Later, they went to the same parties, fought over the same boys, made peace, graduated in the same class, and moved to the States at the same time. Amy does not remember exactly when they first met. Stella has been there from the beginning.

Amy's family was not a regular family. She had an American father, and no kid with an American father was considered a 'regular' kid in Italy. Everybody looked at this circumstance as something exotic and very chic. When he came to visit, Amy would parade him in front of her schoolmates as a creature from another planet.

It was the end of the fifties, and Amy was ten years old. The planet 'America' was basking in all its glory. Images of smiling GIs entering Italian cities devastated by a brutal war were still on the minds of many, those indelible images from news reels that some fifteen years earlier had filled the movie screens and the pages of illustrated magazines. In those days, they had stirred deep emotions and feelings of gratitude among the people. And not only that, people shared a sense of awe for those guys who looked so strong and healthy and smart and outgoing compared to the gaunt faces and desolate looks of the local folks, an army of demigods with good white teeth, bestowing a cornucopia of chocolates, nylons, and ballpoint pens upon a destitute population.

But for the kids of the industrial boom, who saw those war pictures as historical documents of a remote past, the planet 'America' consisted of the mythical Far West, cowboys and

Indians movies, Mickey Mouse and the Disney menagerie, chewing gum, baseball caps, Coca-Cola, and the latest musical craze—rock and roll. It was cool to look American, a popular song told them. It went like this:

> *Tu vuò fà l'americano, mericano, mericano,*
> *ma sei nato in Italy...*
> *Sient'a me, nun ce sta nient'a fà.*
> *Okay, napulità.*
> (You want to look American, merican, merican,
> But you were born in Italy...
> Listen to me, nothing to be done.
> Okay, Neapolitàn.)

As a result of the Marshall Plan, Italy was catapulted out of a dormant economy still anchored in the nineteenth century, into the world of mass consumption. Where centuries of wars and occupations had failed, American culture won. It encroached upon tradition and marked the beginning of a huge transformation. The transformation was not just economic, but also social and psychological, as is often the case.

Because of her American father, Amy was considered privileged among the kids. But in a nice way. It was sort of an admiration devoid of envy. In fact, you can only envy someone who is like you, just luckier. Not someone who belongs in another sphere. They felt she was different, that's all. And, although they looked up to her and sought her company, they never felt totally at ease. And so, she had no friends. Only Stella.

One summer at Villa Flora, Amy and Stella were lying in the meadow outside the gardens, in the thick grass that would soon be cut to make hay. The hilly landscape of the Piedmont countryside south of Turin, renowned for its fine wines, was displayed before their eyes, like in the frescoes adorning the walls of the villa. The meadow was on a slope, rolling down gently to the bottom of the hill. Wild flowers provided splashes of color on the green field, hundreds of nuances of purple, blue, yellow and white. Beyond the meadow were the vineyards, on smaller hills, one after another in an undulating succession, like the waves of the ocean. The sun was at its zenith. The heat energized the earth and made every color more vivid, every smell more intense, every buzz more vibrant.

"Are you really leaving next week?" Stella asked.

"Of course."

"But do you *really* want to go?"

"I can't wait. Dad said he'll take me all over the States and show me those places he sent me postcards of. I'm so excited. Why don't you come along?"

"I can't go."

"Why?"

Stella rolled over and lay flat on her back, then opened her arms to cover as much ground as possible. She took in a deep breath of air, dense with the fragrance of grass and the rich smell of earth.

"I feel like little shoots are growing out of my body and making their way down into the earth. Right here. It's the sun that makes them sprout. And I'm tied down and becoming grass and flowers myself."

"Come on! Cut it out. I know you're good in composition at school, but… the fact is you're just scared. Scared of going so far away from home. I bet the minute you get there you'd start crying because you miss mommy."

"Amy…!"

That was Rosa calling from the alley that led up to the villa.

"Amy…! Lunch is ready. Hurry up, don't make *signora* Amelia wait."

Signora Amelia was Amy's grandmother. Amy was supposed to be named after her, but at the last minute mother decided that Amelia was not good enough, and named her America. Yes, *America*. Was it a way to influence her destiny? She didn't know. But she liked it. She really did.

"Coming!" Amy shouted back, as she and Stella sprinted to race each other uphill.

"I can't go," Stella repeated. Meaning to America, not to lunch.

Well, Amy did go and had a great time. She had graduated from fifth grade that year and there had been some discussion in the family on whether she should enroll in an American school for a year abroad. But mother thought that she was too young and that a summer vacation would be more than enough for her first American experience. As it turned out, Amy never had her year abroad. She had other vacations, though, and eventually moved over there to enroll in graduate school. But that first summer in New York was memorable, and nothing in all the ensuing years could ever compare to it. Upon her return, Amy recorded that experience in her diary, a cute little notebook daddy gave her to develop her love for writing.

> *To be around dad was a lot of fun. He called me names I had never heard before and that made me laugh—sweetie, sweetie pie, sweetheart. I thought he made them up. But most of the time he just called me, girl. I loved that. Simple, direct, without sugar. It implied a rapport of camaraderie. Especially when he said it with a wink, as in: Alright, girl? Wink.*
>
> *I thought he was very handsome, with longish blond hair and a mischievous smirk. And he had a way with women they found irresistible. In fact, it was almost impossible to have a private moment with him. There was always one girlfriend or other around, at home and at the office.*
>
> *Home for him was a large penthouse on two levels on the Upper East Side with a view on the park. He lived on the top level which had huge rooms, floor-to-ceiling windows, and even a swimming pool on the deck. On the lower level were the offices of L&N Publishers. Dad was the boss. Actually, he was the founder and sole owner. Why L&N then, I asked,*

*what does it stand for? He said that L stood for Lawrence/
Larry, which was his name, and N, for None in Particular.
It just sounded good. Dad was like that, he liked to tease. But
I thought that, perhaps, he needed someone to stand by him.*

*A private elevator opened straight into the reception
room arriving from the lobby fifty floors below, in fifty seconds. To me, that elevator was sort of a fair ride. And I would
go up and down up and down, just for the fun of it. The
office suite was very busy, with its team of tweed-jacketed,
pipe-smoking editors—the intellectual type—engulfed in
loud discussion with each other, and a large staff of pretty
women. After work, colleagues would show up in the living
quarters for drinks and conversation. The one that came upstairs most often was Molly, the only woman editor. She had
a great athletic body—she had been a swimming champion
in college—and on weekends she spent hours in the pool doing laps. When she was done, she would give me lessons. At
the end of the summer, I was an expert swimmer. I liked her
a lot, and so did dad.*

*But at times, dad felt that he needed a break from Molly,
the pretty staff, the office, the authors, the critics, the book
launching parties, and the many demands on his private and
public life. At those times, he would look at me and say: Now
we're going to disappear. Just the two of us. Alright, girl?
Wink.*

*Once we disappeared for two weeks. Dad kept his word
and took me to all the places I had seen on postcards, "from
sea to shining sea." He sang for me while driving his Cor-
vette convertible toward the Rocky Mountains and beyond.
We went as far as California where he grew up and where
he still had the Santa Barbara mansion he inherited from his
parents.*

All this was dazzling for a kid her age. But even in her
enchantment she would, at times, think of mother back home

and feel a sting of nostalgia. Amy wondered why she categorically refused to come and live here. Anna, that was her name, said her life was in Italy, especially her life as an artist, because she could not grow and express herself outside of her own environment. She had achieved some recognition as a young artist, and now her works were internationally known. At the beginning of her career, she had a show in New York. It was on that occasion that Anna and Larry met.

The gallery owner had commissioned the catalogue from L&N Publishers, and at the opening he introduced Larry to the artist. Larry was a big hit with women. Anna was very beautiful. Tall and slender, she moved with the grace of a reed wafted by a light breeze, and her classic features possessed an inner radiance. Larry was smitten. So, that night the two of them ended up in the penthouse. Anna did not leave the next day, as she was scheduled to, or the next week, or even the next month. She stayed in New York much longer than she had planned. When she finally left, Larry followed her and spent several months in Italy. He went back after Amy was born, when he became convinced that Anna would never agree to marry him.

When Amy returned from that first summer vacation, she was bombarded with questions—Tell me about America. It must be fabulous over there. What did you see?—And she must have repeated her story a hundred times, about the swimming pool on the deck, the fifty-floor elevator, the tropical greenhouse in the lobby with its parrots and streams, surfing in the Pacific Ocean, and other marvels. Stella, in particular, wanted to go over the details time and again. They practiced English together, spending long hours on their favorite bench in the rose garden at Villa Flora, reading a wide range of novels from Jane Austen to Mark Twain. Amy was pretty fluent by then. She made a lot of progress during her summer months in New York, and, of course, it helped that she had an English nanny as a child. On the other hand, this contributed to her strange accent, an odd combination of native Italian, stylish British, and ordinary New Yorkese.

"Here we are, miss. Where should I drop you off?" The cabbie wakes her up from her reverie.

"Can you pull up by the pizza place, over there? D'you see the sign, Santa Lucia?"

"Lucheeah...is this how you say it in Italy?! It sounds pretty. Isn't it misspelled on the sign?"

Jeez, something's lost in translation, Amy thinks, and I don't have the time for a language lesson.

"Here, keep the change. And go take your kid to school."

"Thank you, miss. It's nice of you..."

...and something else she can't hear. She's already running, always on the run.

She catches a glimpse of her image in a shop window. She likes what she sees. Slender figure, good legs, bumpy curls, a focused gaze, a smart designer outfit... Overall, a youngish, sexy woman. She'll turn fifty-four in a month and she looks even better than the glamorous boomers on the cover of AARP Magazine. I'm gonna have a big party, she promises herself.

The door to the pizzeria is locked. She has to go in from the parking lot in the back. Rosa is surprised to see her.

"Hi, beauty!" She actually says: *Ciao, bellezza,* because she prefers to speak Italian to her. They hug and kiss. "What happened? Did you fall off the bed?"

"Sort of. Way too early for me. Last night I worked until 2 a.m."

"You need a good cup of coffee. Real Italian espresso."

Rosa goes behind the counter on which a massive Illy coffee maker towers in all its glory of shiny chrome, black levers, bending tubes, hissing spouts, and steam puffs. As a result of her skillful operation, the machine releases a precious drop of concentrated coffee in each of two tiny cups. Rosa brings them to the table and they sit down.

The dining room is large and bright, with tasteful Mediterranean decor—white walls, terracotta floor, dark wood furniture, and ceramic panels with landscapes of the Amalfi coast imported from the region. On one side, French doors lead to a patio lined with potted lemon and orange trees. On the other side, a wood-burning oven is in full view.

"I had not seen it after the renovation," Amy says, looking around. "It's really nice. Simple and elegant."

"You should tell Chris. He's the one who designed it and supervised the work." Chris is Rosa's son, a successful architect and the owner of a hip design studio, the first in the family to graduate from college. Rosa continues, "It took him a long time to convince his father that the place needed a facelift. Joe didn't want to hear of it. He liked it the way his parents set it up fifty years ago, with Formica table tops and an electric oven tucked away in the back of the kitchen. But now, he too is happy with the results. Business has been terrific."

II

A flashback

Joe Tornese was born in New York in the early 1930s, a second-generation son of Italian immigrants from a village south of Naples. His parents came to the U.S. as kids, with their families, after WWI. In 1921 the U.S. had resumed its immigration program, after a brief interruption due to the war, and had passed the first Immigration Quota Law to control the huge demand from people desperate to escape the dismal living conditions in a Europe devastated by the conflict. Joe's grandparents and their children were among the 560,971 immigrants admitted to the United States that year. Joe's mother, known as Mamma Lucia among the pizzeria's patrons, is still alive at age eighty-nine and keeps telling the same story that Amy has heard dozens of times.

"*È stata la miseria, bella mia.* We were starving, you know? You think we would leave if we were well off? You kiddin'? That was home, family, friends, the graves in the cemetery... Hell, no. We would not leave. But we were starving. The land we worked belonged to the baron, don Ferdinando, that sonnabitch God forgive him. He had acres and acres of land, and we and other hands worked just a small piece each family. Still, it would have been enough. But at the end of each month, his men came by on horseback, with a wagon, and took all the crop. We sweated on his land and were left with nothing. *Noi a faticà e lui a magnà.* We had no choice but to get on the ship and go seek a better life."

Lucia was nine when the family embarked on their journey to America with their possessions wrapped up in two blankets. Going up the gangplank, the father carried the two big bundles, the mother held two younger sons in her arms, and Lucia walked by her, holding on to her skirt. For three weeks they shared the cramped quarters in the bowels of the ship with dozens of other families. The air was stifling, there were no portholes. They slept on narrow berths, adults and children together. Twice a day they received a meager meal, consisting mainly of soup and stale bread. Many were seasick, others fell seriously ill, two women gave birth before their time. The stench grew more unbearable every day. Lucia was able to sneak out at dusk and venture onto the upper deck. At that time, the first-class passengers and the crew were having dinner, and she could move stealthily around without being seen. On one of her outings, she met a boy about her age, a fellow immigrant who ten years later became her husband.

Lucia went on with her story.

"Down there it was hell. And up on the deck it was heaven. *Un paradiso.* So many stars… and so close. The air was fresh, everything was clean and tidy. Now I had a friend, Rocco, and together we watched the white tail in the water behind the ship that sparkled in the moonlight. That made me forget that I was terribly hungry. We also found a spot where we could look through a window and see the large dining room with beautiful people, women in silk dresses with jewelry in the hair and around the neck, drinking and dancing. Rocco said that in America we, too, will be living like this.

"When the ship entered the harbor at the end of the journey, they let us all out to the lower deck to have a view of the land that we would call home from now on. I saw the big statue of the Lady with a long gown and a crown on the head, and I thought she looked very elegant and impressive, like those women in the dining room, but more strong and powerful, and I felt she was there to welcome me, like she was saying, 'Hello, Lucia. *Benvenuta*. Come on in. Now you belong with us.' And I realized that Rocco was right."

As it turned out, Lucia's expectations did not materialize in the way she and Rocco had envisioned. Nevertheless, in the end they were able to attain a modest measure of the American Dream. It was not easy.

After docking, the immigrants were corralled into the reception facilities on Ellis Island, where they endured a month of interviews, physical exams, background investigations of their criminal and political records, and other humiliating but necessary procedures to ascertain that they were fit to become citizens of this privileged nation. Many did not pass the test, for one reason or another, and were sent back home on the next available ship. They were crushed, their dream was shattered. Lucia's parents were gripped by fear that this may happen to them as well. So, they made an extra effort to be on their best behavior, do exactly as they were told, give all the right answers, and smile a lot. Perhaps this helped, or perhaps they just got lucky. At the end of the month, the family received a pack of newly-stamped papers and was admitted into the U.S.A.

They settled in a small one-bedroom apartment, on the fifth floor of a tenement not far from the pizzeria's current location. They got the apartment through St. Christopher Church, which provided assistance to the newly-arrived. The parish priest explained that the church was named after the saint who once carried Baby Jesus across the water, and was therefore considered the patron saint of the immigrants.

There were many Italians in the neighborhood, and that made it easier to get started. They gave each other emotional and material support in a city that would have otherwise felt terrifying—a huge, alien world where everybody spoke a language they did not understand. Through a *cumpà*, a hometown fellowman who had been in New York for a few years, Lucia's father soon got a job in construction. Her mother worked as a cleaning woman for a hotel chain while a next-door neighbor took care of the younger kids together with her own grandchildren.

Lucia enrolled in first grade because she had not had any schooling back home. And so did Rocco, even though he was two years older. They lived on the same street, and in the morning went to school together. They had to be careful to avoid the back alleys. Those were dangerous places because of the rival gangs that roamed the neighborhood—Italian, Irish and Jewish. But Rocco knew how to keep out of trouble and, if needed, how to kick a bully in the crotch. They soon learned to speak English well enough, and also to read and write in that language because, as Rocco said, this is what it takes to get rich in America. However, notwithstanding their best efforts, they never acquired native fluency. Their choice of words, their turn of phrase, their intonation would forever be a bit off. And their accent remained markedly Southern Italian, because at home this was the only language their parents spoke. This branded them inexorably as "not quite" American, even in the eyes of the best-intentioned people, and triggered the dreaded question—Where are you from?—at each and every first casual encounter. On occasion, they were met with hostility. More often, it was a sympathetic but overly concerned stare that made them feel diminished, as if the person had just learned that they suffered from some disability and needed help.

After graduation from primary school, they went to work; Lucia in a textile factory, and Rocco in a diner that belonged to an uncle of his. Every third Sunday, Rocco had the day off, and the two of them took the train to Coney Island and spent the afternoon at Luna Park. On the way to the station, they held hands and Rocco sang to her in his Neapolitan-accented English:

We'll take a trip up to the moon
For that is the place for a lark.
So meet me down at Luna, Lena,
Down at Luna Park.

They splurged a few pennies on cotton candy and lemonade and walked among those mesmerizing attractions—the
giant Wonder Wheel, the Cyclone roller coaster, the dizzy-
ing merry-go-rounds, brightly colored and scintillating with
hundreds of lights. They laughed at the grotesque images on
the freak show posters—"Marian: Headless Girl From Lon-
don," "Winsome Winnie: Fat Pretty And Jolly," "Zip & Pip:
2 Georgia Peaches," "Smallest Grown Ups On Earth"… And,
although they could not afford the ticket for a ride or a show,
they were happy all the same to watch the action and listen to
the music.

When Lucia turned twenty, her father consented to their
marriage. For the occasion he spent most of his savings of ten
years. They had a reception at the church for the extended
family, some fifty relatives on each side, with wine and food
catered by Rocco's uncle. Lucia had received a few yards of
white silk from the textile factory as a wedding gift, and her
mother sewed her a beautiful bridal gown. She looked splendid in that dress. Dancing with Rocco, she felt like the princess in an American fairy tale of her own. Rocco's uncle acted
as the MC and toasted the couple repeatedly, with wishes of a
bright future and *figli maschi* (male children), which according
to tradition was regarded as the most desirable and luckiest
of outcomes.

They were not disappointed because one year later Joe
was born. As for the bright future, it had to wait another
fifteen years. It was 1933, and they were already deep into
the Great Depression. Four years earlier, the nation, and the
world, looked in dismay at the collapse of the stock market,
and now pinned their hopes on President Roosevelt for guid-
ance and reassurance.

Unemployment in the U.S. rose to 25 percent. Lucia's father lost his job with the private developer he had been working for, and joined the lines of the unemployed that grew longer and longer every day. The textile factory where Lucia worked had to shut down and lay off the entire work force. She, Rocco and little Joe moved in with her parents in order to save on the rent and help the family. They slept on cots in the kitchen, while Lucia's parents and her younger brothers shared the bedroom. To make ends meet, Lucia joined her mother on the hotel cleaning team.

Rocco, on the other hand, managed to keep his job at the diner, and was even promoted from busboy to cook. It was thanks to his talent for pizza-making that the diner could survive through those dismal years. Pizza was born in Naples as a food for the poor—who knows when? Perhaps as soon as tomatoes where imported from America in the sixteenth century. At that time, it consisted of flat bread, tomatoes, olive oil, and oregano. No cheese. Cheese was added later, when pizza was already on its way to acquiring status as a folk cuisine specialty. The original version could be produced and sold for a few cents. That is what Rocco understood. His pizza was a bargain that most people could afford. The sign in the window declared: *You CAN'T afford NOT to buy it!* In fact, Rocco explained, it's darn cheap, it fills an empty stomach and, on top of everything, it tastes soooo good—even if he had to substitute corn oil for olive oil and use tomato paste in the winter instead of fresh tomatoes.

Unlike other businesses, the diner was doing well, and Rocco's uncle was able to pay him a decent salary. That is, until they received a visit from the local godfather.

Don Vincent Marrano sat down at a corner table with two of his henchmen, their backs to the wall, their faces partly obscured by fedora hats. He ordered pizza for himself. The other two remained vigilant while he was eating. Afterwards, he asked to talk to Rocco's uncle:

"*Chist'è robba buona.* This is good stuff. You're providing a good service to the people in the neighborhood. I want you to be able to continue. So, I offer you my protection. From now on, you won't have to worry about nothing. If there's a problem, we'll take care of it. *Parola mia.* You have my word."

A handshake, and the deal was sealed—with or without the uncle's consent. At the end of each month, the two thugs in fedora hats came by to collect the money, leaving almost nothing for Rocco's salary—just like the baron's men back home would come and get our crop, that sonnabitch God forgive him, commented Mamma Lucia in her tale.

Then, one day, Lucia's father came home with good news: he had been hired for one of the big construction projects that came about with the New Deal. That evening he went out to celebrate with some buddies of his who had had the same good fortune. Two hours later, the police knocked on the door to notify the family that someone should go to the morgue to identify the body. The police never found out what happened exactly. A brawl... an attempt to break a fight... to help a friend... the knife missed the intended target... he got the blow. Nobody came forward to provide any information, and those who were interrogated kept their mouth shut. After a perfunctory investigation, the case was closed. Not for don Vince Marrano, though. Eyewitnesses in his service identified the killer, and the guy was promptly gunned down in broad daylight in front of Rocco's diner. This was don Vince's way to declare his protection publicly with a spectacular gesture.

To further tighten the grip on Rocco's family, don Vince hired Lucia's younger brothers—with or without the family's consent. They were just fourteen and fifteen years old, and their job consisted of keeping watch during the mob's operations—usually, the operations involved moving alcohol cargoes from the warehouse to their network of speakeasies. The two unsuspected lookouts would alert the gang if the police were closing in. Although Prohibition had ended the previous year, U.S. federal law imposed numerous limitations and heavy taxation on the production and distribution of distilled spirits, and organized crime was still thriving on bootlegging. As the brothers grew up, their level of involvement increased, and at age twenty they were full-fledged members of the racket. This put Rocco in the awkward position of having to pay protection money to his brothers-in-law. But the brothers, discretly, never showed up at the diner, and within the family nobody ever talked about business. So, on the surface, they were all friends.

By the end of the thirties, the brothers were able to provide a decent living for their mother. She and Lucia quit their cleaning jobs and the family moved to a nice house in Brooklyn, where everyone had a room of their own. Even Joe, who at the time was eight years old. He needed his own space, because every year on his birthday don Vince would send him a magnificent gift, something a working-class kid could only dream of. One year, it was a rocking horse, lusciously decorated like the ponies on the merry-go-round. The next year, it was an electric train with a railway network that covered half of his room. More recently, it was a bicycle that looked like those for grown-ups in all details. Joe was ecstatic and felt grateful to "uncle" Vince. On the other hand, something about the man made him uncomfortable. He sensed that his father disapproved of those gifts. When they were alone, Rocco would suddenly hug him tight and say something like, "This stuff's not for free... I'm so sorry I can't do anything to stop it..."

Rocco and Lucia had no other children after Joe. And so, Rocco's desire to shield his son from the Mafia occupied all his thoughts. He even made a vow to St. Christopher that he would help renovate the church if the saint would free them from under the thumb of the mob. However, deep down he doubted that St. Christopher would be able to work that miracle. Affiliation with the Marrano family was for life. The few who had tried to terminate it had their lives terminated instead. But then, something happened. It is not clear whether St. Christopher wanted so badly to have his church renovated, or whether it was a mere coincidence, but a month later Lucia's brothers were killed in a shootout with the police. Lucia and her mother were stricken with grief. But Rocco breathed a sigh of relief. At least one link was broken, although the chain had not completely fallen off. Don Vince offered his condolences to the mother together with a generous lump sum for compensation.

That money came in handy in the next four years, when another major event disrupted the normal course of things. The vicious Japanese attack at Pearl Harbor propelled the United States into a war that had expanded from Europe to Africa, and now Asia.

Rocco was among the first to join the Army as a volunteer, moved by patriotic spirit. He thought that among his comrades-in-arms he would finally feel like a "true" American. He was thirty-one years old at the time and had no military training, but he was accepted immediately because of his bilingual background. The Army needed interpreters for its daring European mission.

A sense of duty and sacrifice in the service of the country's ideals of freedom and democracy inspired everybody. Many young guys in the neighborhood, who were drafted, looked forward to the great adventure with enthusiasm and high expectations. The minorities—immigrants and blacks—felt redeemed by a sense of pride. But even in upper-scale America, where nobody needed redemption, and where money and connections could have been used to avoid the call, most young men left behind families and jobs to perform their patriotic duty.

Only a few tried to dodge the draft. It was after all a war, where one could get killed. One of those was Frank Marrano, Vince's son. He was twenty-one and a college drop-out.

For the first time in his criminal career, Vince felt powerless. The military complex was not a field of operations he was familiar with. No matter how hard he tried, he failed to hook up to the higher echelons in the chain of command. Not even his political connections, who could normally be bought for money or persuaded by threat, could help in this case. In the end, Frank had to go. He and Rocco were assigned to the same assault division that would first reach the shores of Italy in the summer of '43.

Before the guys' departure, Vince showed up at Rocco's place. He looked tired and depressed as if he had somehow aged overnight. He sat at the kitchen table, took a glass of wine from Lucia's hands, patted Joe on the head, then looked at Rocco in the eye and said:

"We've known each other for years. I've got to love you as a second son, and will continue to keep your family under my protection when you're gone. But now I want you to do something for me. I want you to keep an eye on my boy when you two are over there. I don't want him to come back in a body bag. Look over him, as if you were his guardian angel. *Dammi la tua parola d'onore.* Your word of honor."

Vince extended his hand. Rocco took it and said:

"*Parola d'onore.*"

The Americans disembarked on the coast of Sicily and joined the British and Canadian forces already on the ground. It took about six weeks for the Allies to secure their positions on the island. In early September, they began their march north through the peninsula. They did not meet a serious resistance for the first two months, because the Italian army had evaporated after the government signed an armistice with the Allies, and the occupying German army had strategically retreated as far as the town of Cassino south of Rome. But Rocco took his guardianship job seriously, and made sure that Frank had plenty to eat every day, even sacrificing part of his own ration, and a comfortable place to sleep at night.

When the Allies arrived in Naples, at the beginning of October, they were prepared for a big battle to liberate that main military and commercial port. But, to their surprise, the local population had already liberated itself in a bloody uprising that lasted four days, and there was not a single German soldier left in town. So far so good, Frank thought, there's nothing so terrible about this war, and spent a few days in the city spending his money generously on girls and local food, offered on the black market at astronomically high prices. The city was devastated and on its knees, and the people were desperate to exploit whatever opportunity the new powers would bring.

Frank began to get a true sense of the war when the army reached the German fortifications at the foot of Monte Cassino. The road north to Rome was barred by the formidable Gustav Line, which extended from the Tyrrhenian to the Adriatic coasts. It consisted of trenches, gun pits, concrete bunkers, turreted machine-gun platforms, barbed wire, and minefields, and employed fifteen German divisions. Monte Cassino dominated the entrance to the Liri Valley, through which ran the main highway. On top of the mountain was a sixth-century abbey, believed to be a German post. To make things worse, it was now the middle of November, there were several feet of snow on the ground, and the sub-zero temperature made it extremely difficult to engage the enemy. Frank felt miserable and relied heavily on Rocco for support—even in battle, where he would take cover crouching behind his guardian's back. At the camp, Rocco would manage to get him a thermos of hot coffee and fetch an extra blanket to keep him warm.

For six long months the allied forces fought valiantly on the impregnable slopes of Monte Cassino. They assaulted the Gustav defenses four times. In February, American bombers recklessly destroyed the ancient abbey in an action meant to help the ground troops. Unfortunately, it made things worse. As it turned out, the Germans were not garrisoned there, but after the bombing they took up positions in the ruins, finding protection among the rubble. Only at the end of May, with the arrival of the spring, were the Allies able to gather twenty divisions for a major assault. And they broke through the Gustav Line.

During this decisive action, Frank stepped on a landmine and lost his legs. He wanted to avoid the thick of the battle and took a detour through a clearing in the woods, thinking of rejoining his comrades later, when the fire subsided. Unaware, he entered a minefield. He would have bled to death in that secluded spot if it were not for Rocco. At the end of a heroic attack against an artillery post, Rocco realized that Frank was missing. He retraced his steps and found his charge agonizing in a pool of blood. Although he himself was wounded in a shoulder, Rocco managed to carry Frank on his back to the nearest field hospital, where the medics saved his life.

Frank was sent home with the first available transport, while Rocco continued his painful march north, from battle to battle, from victory to final victory.

In January '46, New York gave the returning troops a heroes' welcome—a glorious Victory Parade along Fifth Avenue, with marching bands, flags hanging from every building, a ticker tape blizzard, and thousands of women with open arms eager to hug and kiss the warriors.

The war ended, at least in the Western hemisphere, and the peace began—and with the peace, the most extraordinary period of prosperity.

Rocco's uncle decided to retire and enjoy his senior years on the Florida beaches. He left the diner to Rocco because he had no direct heirs. Under Rocco's management, the old diner was renamed Pizzeria Santa Lucia, and acquired a new identity and a new clientele. "Italian" was no longer just an ethnic qualifier, it became a commercial label. And, yes, mozzarella cheese became a pizza topping— and not only cheese, but pepperoni, sausage, ham, olives, anchovies, mushrooms, and more and more… In the emerging consumer society, *the more the better* was a fundamental principle.

Rocco felt pretty good about the business and about his family. Lucia worked at the counter and Joe, who was fifteen, tended tables after school. Only one thing still bothered him. He was determined to get rid of the racket once and for all. When the two henchmen showed up punctually at the end of the month, Rocco refused to pay, and the next day took his courage in both hands and went to see don Vincent Marrano.

A high wall surrounded the Marrano property out in the countryside. A wrought-iron gate gave access to the alley that cut through the woods and led to a villa in Renaissance style. The gate was locked, and Rocco stood there, uncertain of what to do. A man came out of the guardhouse and asked who he was. Then went back inside to make a phone call. Finally, he opened the gate and escorted Rocco to the mansion.

Don Vince was sitting behind a monumental desk in his study. Everything in the room was oversized—the leather chairs, the fireplace, the chandelier, the vast vista on the lake. Rocco was overwhelmed and felt very small. Vince pointed to a chair across from the desk and began to speak.

"I'm glad to see you, although I heard you treated my boys pretty badly last night. I should be angry with you. However, I'm a man of honor. And I'm indebted to you big time. You saved my son's life. Frank is now a broken man, on a wheelchair, dependent on nurses, and addicted to drugs that are supposed to alleviate his deep depression. He's a total wreck. But he's alive, and I'm grateful to you for that. I want to pay off my debt. Ask me anything you want—money, power, influence. Anything. Tell me. *Parla*."

Rocco spoke in a firm, unemotional voice.

"Don Vince, I have only one request: please, get out of our lives. Forget about us, as if we never met. Leave us alone. If I never hear from you again, I'll consider your debt repaid a thousand times."

Vince was silent for a long time. His eyes closed, his jaws clenched. Then, he took a deep breath and spoke.

"I've never done this for anyone. My friends are friends for life... But I'm an honorable man, and I intend to honor my word. You'll have your wish."

He got up, walked around the desk, grabbed Rocco by the shoulders, pulled him up, and kissed him on both cheeks.

Rocco never heard from don Vince again. Several years later, he learned from the newspapers that the mobster Vincent Marrano had finally been arrested and convicted for tax evasion. The prosecutor had been trying for years to charge him with more serious crimes, but had not been able to gather enough evidence. Not long after the trial, don Vince died in jail—allegedly, of a heart attack.

The pizzeria gradually became a favorite spot for the well-to-dos from uptown in search of a touch of folklore. In the mid-sixties it acquired the license to sell wine and greatly increased in popularity. Now it had a jukebox that played the Four Seasons nonstop. Frankie Valli himself occasionally showed up with members of the band, and there was a photo on the wall of Joe toasting them. Joe was in his early thirties and a partner in the business. To learn more about wine, he took a tour organized by the *Associazione Viticultori d'Italia*, an association of Italian wine producers who wanted to promote their products in the U.S.

For the first time in his life, Joe set foot on an airplane. Rocco drove him to the airport in his station wagon, wondering all the way whether St. Christopher would now modernize and protect transatlantic passengers in the air, as well as on water.

Joe landed safely in Rome and joined the other wine sellers and restaurateurs from all over the States. After touring the Frascati hills and the picturesque wine zones of the south, the group headed north, passing through the Chianti countryside and reaching the fertile vineyards of the Piedmont region.

The tour organizers had included visits to large industrial establishments as well as to specialized small producers. One of these was the Villa Flora winery, famous for its ruby-red, floral-flavored, medium-bodied Grignolino. After having tasted the specialties of other wineries—the robust, berry-flavored, full-bodied Barolo, and the sweet, aromatic Moscato—Joe fell for Grignolino. The perfect match for pizza, as he put it. On that occasion Joe met Rosa.

The visitors to the winery were routinely treated to a brief tour of the eighteenth-century villa and its gardens. *Signora* Amelia had first resisted this intrusion. Her family had always kept a clear demarcation line between their private space and the winery down in the valley. But the manager had convincingly argued that the visits would help to increase the business, and in the end she relented. The world was changing and business was gradually encroaching on everything. However, she would not come out and greet the visitors. She stood firm on that point. And so, she put Rosa in charge of supervising the wine-tasting reception and of seeing to it that the group leave promptly soon after.

It was mid-July and the gardens let off fireworks of blossoms—periwinkles, daisies, forget-me-nots, lilies, peonies, fuchsias and nasturtiums artistically arranged in manicured flower beds, perfectly trimmed hydrangea shrubs around the fountain, jasmine edges along the alleys, and thick clusters of wisteria climbing up the southern wall. The rose garden was not in full view, secluded behind a row of cypresses and surrounded by a delicate colonnade, but the intense fragrance of hundreds of blooms of all possible varieties floated in the air and travelled all the way up to the terrace where the visitors were standing. The terrace extended outside the grand hall in the back of the villa. Stone banisters with neo-classical statues of the four seasons surrounded it. On one side, steps lead to the gardens.

The visitors were in awe of that luxuriant spectacle, and

eagerly clicked their cameras left and right, leaning on the banisters because they were not allowed down the steps. A young man in the group, the one who spoke Italian (with a terrible accent), was more interested in Rosa than in the surroundings. He followed her around like her shadow while she was attending to her duties. He was the last one to leave, lingering at the door to talk to her at length. That night they met in town and Joe stayed over for another couple of days. Eventually, he came back a few months later to marry her. Rosa left Villa Flora, and *signora* Amelia lost her most valued maid.

III

New York 2001

"For sure, the place now has a very sleek look. But I feel a bit nostalgic for the old place with its retro charm. Look at that picture... Aren't they cute?"

Amy points to a photo on the wall, picturing Rocco and Lucia in '46 in front of their pizza joint. They are in their Sunday best: Rocco in a dark suit custom-made by the tailor on the corner who knew how to make a man look smart, and Lucia in a light dress with a floral pattern, slingbacks with a high wedge, and a small hat on her shoulder-length black hair—two proud business owners and respected citizens.

"They earned every bit of what they've got, the hard way," Rosa says. "Rocco remained loyal to this country until his very last day. He used to tell us, still in his heavy Southern Italian accent, 'Look, here money doesn't grow on trees. But it's the only country in the world where everyone has the opportunity to plant his own tree.' We owe them a great deal. Joe had it easy. Having been born here he never experienced the humiliation of being an immigrant and, of course, he is a native speaker. I laugh at him when he speaks Italian with his thick Yankee accent... As for Chris, he doesn't even try."

"Yeah, Joe's funny. But you're amazing. You learned English so well, you're almost flawless."

"It must be a natural gift. I never learned it in school. You know my story, the nuns at the orphanage gave me just a basic education, and at eighteen I went to work at your grandma's... Then I came here, not as a poor person but as the wife of a solid citizen, a businessman, and this gave me a new confidence, and so I learned the language easily... But, enough talking about me. Tell me about yourself, honey. Haven't seen you in ages. How's life?"

"I'm fine. Very busy. Lately, I've been working on a manuscript that requires a lot of time and labor. In fact, that's why I dropped by today. I wanted to ask you if you remember..."

The door to the office flies open, and Joe rushes out, highly distressed:

"Rosa! Rosa, come quickly! Something's happened... It's in the news, live. Oh, Amy, hi! Hurry, both of you... You must see this."

They rush to the office. On the TV screen they see a scene out of a disaster movie. The North Tower of the World Trade Center looks like a factory chimney. A plume of dark, dense smoke is gushing out a huge gap at about the 80th floor, wide and thin like a throat cut. The smoke snakes up to the sky and expands into a massive cloud that tops the tower.

"A plane hit the tower... three minutes ago, at 8:46... we don't have the facts... it could have been an accident..." The reporter is desperately trying to make sense of the event.

The video runs again from the beginning. A clear blue sky, a plane flying directly into the tower, the impact is horrendous, the plane remains lodged in the building. "Holy shit!" An anonymous voice from someone watching the scene has been recorded on the soundtrack. "Holy shit!... Holy shit!" Three times, in disbelief.

"What's happening?" Rosa asks, not expecting an answer. They are mesmerized, their eyes glued to the screen, when a second plane is spotted. It approaches with the deliberate trajectory of a kamikaze. It hits the South Tower at about the same height and crashes into the building with a spectacular explosion. It is 9:03. Flames and smoke gush out of the wounded building. By now, it is clear to them that they are not watching an accident.

"We're under attack... An act of terrorism... Unconfirmed reports talk of an Al-Qaeda operation," the broken voice of the commentator informs them. "All of Manhattan has been sealed off, bridges and tunnels have been shut down. The airports are closed, the whole airspace has been declared a no-fly zone."

The two towers are burning. First responders are already at the scene. People from inside the towers call 911. They place frantic calls: "I'm burning up. Help me! Hurry, please!" Firefighters enter the towers' inferno. They make their way upstairs, as high up as possible. As they approach the 70th floor, they have to stop. Above it, it's a flaming furnace. They help the survivors to evacuate the lower floors.

A steady stream of people emerges from the buildings. Ambulances collect the injured. Many suffer from extensive burns. The anchor says that a huge fireball plunged down the elevator shaft and blew out the door when it hit the ground floor, engulfing the crowd that was running toward the exit. Those who can walk on their own ignore the reporters that want to interview them, anxious to run away from the mayhem. The Plaza in front of the towers is covered with high-heel women's shoes left behind.

"My God! They're jumping from the 100th floor!" Rosa, with tears in her eyes, clasps her hands against her mouth.

They cannot believe what they see. Haunted by the fire, people rush to the windows, seeking an illusory escape. They jump. Hundreds of bodies perform a tragic dance in the air and crash to the ground amid a cascade of flaming debris.

It is 9:37. The BREAKING NEWS signal flashes in red across the screen. The scene shifts from New York to Arlington, Virginia, where a third plane has just crashed into the west wall of the Pentagon. They watch the replay. The plane is approaching at minimal altitude like for a landing, but going full speed. When it hits, it takes down the entire wall, leaving a gaping black hole in the white stone perimeter. The hole quickly fills up with smoke and flames. Now they are watching it live. Here, too, rescue squads arrive in no time. They help people out of the building, lay the injured down on the lawn for the ambulances to pick them up. There are not many survivors.

A voice over reports the news as it happens: "Air force jets are patrolling the space over the nation's capital... The authorities fear an attack on Washington, DC... A United Airline flight, Flight 93, apparently has been hijacked... passengers have reached relatives on their cell phones...The White House has been evacuated, as well as all the buildings in the vicinities... The Capitol building and the Congressional offices have also been evacuated. We were told that the President was not in Washington this morning and he is now in a safe place. He will address the nation later in the day..." Then, abruptly, "Back to the New York studio. An emergency situation has developed there..."

"What else could still possibly happen?" asks Joe. He keeps his arms around Rosa. She clings to him. They draw strength from each other. Their mutual support also rubs off on Amy.

Back to New York. It is 9:59. The South Tower collapses. It implodes and crumbles like a castle of cards. A gigantic cloud of dust and smoke engulfs the area. The media are caught in that dense mass. For a while the screen is pitch black. Voices emerge from the dark: "Holy crap! It's gone... the whole tower!" Gradually, the image returns.

A huge wave of white dust rushes through the streets. It rises up sixty feet. It fills the space. It runs over everything on its path. It pushes the crowd of survivors from behind like a raging torrent, like a gaseous tsunami. The debris trapped in the dust hit people like bullets.

A reporter emerges from the cloud, whitened with a thick coat of dust, coughing but still talking: "Many people remain in the rubble, crushed under concrete slabs and steel beams, their bodies minced and burned, unrecognizable, unrecoverable. Among them are many brave firefighters, and members of the Port Authority Police and of NYPD. They are heroes."

Blinded and choked, people run away from the unleashed fury of the dust wave and seek shelter in doorways, stores, cafés... Trinity Church, a few blocks away, soon becomes a recovery center.

People keep running. They move up Broadway in a steady stream. Soon they are outside the pizzeria. Joe rushes to open the door. The dining room and the patio fill up with a pack of white ghosts. Some are injured, all are shaken, shocked, exhausted, disoriented, confused, incredulous... Rosa hands out water and food. Amy helps her. Joe goes to fetch blankets and first aid supplies. Then, Chris rushes in from Midtown to join forces with the rest of them, just in time before the area is sealed off.

A piece of news that was lost in the confusion is now being repeated on the radio: "At 10:06, UA Flight 93 crashed in a field in Pennsylvania, south-east of Pittsburgh, not far from the town of Shanksville. Apparently, a group of passengers showed extraordinary courage and took on the hijackers. They engaged the terrorists at the controls in the cockpit. Relatives on the phone reported that the plane was rolling wildly before crashing. The plane was allegedly directed toward the Washington Capitol in a suicide mission."

Joe manages to bring a TV set into the dining room. It is 10:28. They witness the collapse of the North Tower. It is like a movie replay, a *déjà vu*, but not for this less horrific—another implosion, another wave of dust, more victims trapped in the rubble, more dead. Survivors keep coming in through the front door. Now, they are everywhere. They sit on blankets on the floor.

By the end of the day everyone is gone, picked up by loved ones, friends, or paramedics. Chris escorts out a few people who had no assistance.

In the empty room, the three of them sit in silence. The TV is still on. At the disaster site the fire has been extinguished, but the ashes are still burning. In the dim daylight the area is a flat, snowy-like landscape. The remains of the towers are contorted skeletons standing out sharply against the white background, Gothic silhouettes from a horror movie set for chiaroscuro effect.

Joe turns off the TV. The three of them get up and walk toward the door. They hug. Amy leaves.

At her desk that night Amy finds it difficult to work. Her eyes wander from the page to the window — a transparent wall, connecting, rather than separating, the interior space to the lights of the big city that never sleeps. One step through the glass, and she would be gliding among the stars of that electric firmament.

She lives in Larry's penthouse. He died recently in a car accident. At seventy-eight, still in love with sport cars. She inherited his estate, and with it the publishing house. She had been working with Larry at L&N for many years as editorial director and, after the accident, she filled his chair as president.

I love New York, Amy thinks... since that far-away summer of my childhood, when I was first struck and forever conquered by its aggressive charm. Today, her city has been violated. Lady Liberty has been raped. She recalls the words of the cabbie that morning, "A pack of mad dogs..." It seems that, in this case, the mad dogs have only been facilitators. The pundits on all TV channels speculate that the mastermind behind this heinous operation is a Saudi by the name of Osama bin Laden, the head of a terrorist organization known as Al-Qaeda.

In the optics of a perverse aesthetics, today's tragic event looks to her like the conclusion of a cycle, the unhappy grand finale of a historical era. And, what is worse, it also looks like an ominous sign at the dawning of a new century, a new millennium.

Amy does not want to speculate about tomorrow. She clicks on *Stella's Story*, brings up the digitized manuscript, and plunges into yesterday.

PART TWO

Yesterday (1967-1985)

Stella's Story Manuscript

Stella's Story: Chapter 1
Los Angeles, 1967

The light filtering through the venetian blinds woke me up like every morning. I looked out the window. The sun was already high, painting our backyard in bright colors. The avocado tree—so green; the hibiscus flowers—so red; the water in the pool—so blue; the fence around the lawn—so white. Another sunny day. So predictable.

It was November. At this time, the hills around Villa Flora disappear in the fog, and down in the valley a light mist that smells of truffles covers everything. My skin, my hair, my mind longed for a quick dip into that mist, just to absorb new sap.

Jim was still asleep. He slept until late in the morning and nothing would wake him up, not even a temblor of the San Andreas Fault. He tenaciously clung to that torpid state as if he dreaded to face the beginning of a new day.

From the living room, the radio reminded me that *"it never rains in Southern California."* Too bad. I put on a bikini and went for a swim. Not in our pool, the size of a soup bowl. In the ocean. The ocean, out there, frightening and majestic.

We lived in Venice. That is, Venice, California. The house was right on the beach. In those days Venice was a funky neighborhood, a favorite hangout of the Flower Children who drifted south after the Summer of Love in San Francisco. But also students and junior faculty with no money lived there. Small run-down bungalows and overgrown yards lined the streets parallel to the beach. Other streets with the same bungalows and cracked sidewalks crossed them perpendicularly, creating a symmetrical grid. Some lots looked abandoned. They were empty, except for a lone gas station or an occasional convenience store with a big sign in the front. Others hosted used car dealerships, festooned all around with a line of red and blue fluttering tags. The closest supermarket was ten blocks away, by the ramp to Highway 1. Huge billboards broke the flatness of the landscape, rising above the roofs and pitching their products in deafening colors. I never really liked it there. I found it difficult to blend with the environment.

I closed the bedroom door behind me. The house was empty. Everyone had already gone out, leaving the breakfast dishes on the kitchen table. Hamlet trotted toward me and rubbed his nose against my legs. He almost threw me off. Not a frail creature like the melancholy prince, this Great Dane was a huge beast, his head reaching above my waist. His dish was the only one still clean. They forgot to feed him. I poured in nondescript brown balls from a 20-pound bag of dog food and added some water. I went out the front door, not bothering to lock it. Door keys were not an item in use. Nobody ever locked the door, day or night, and thefts were a rare occurrence. It was more likely to find a stranger sleeping on the couch than to find something missing. I crossed the front lawn cluttered with folding chairs, sleeping bags, and children's toys, and stepped on the boardwalk.

The boardwalk was narrow, lined with palm trees. It was not commercialized, there were only a few vendors of hot dogs and *chili con carne*. The glamour of Hollywood was miles away. Sunset Boulevard ended up on the Santa Monica beach, well north of Venice.

I found myself a spot on the beach where I could have some privacy, and laid down my towel. Young people in tattered jeans and colorful rags hung out there, strolling leisurely or lying on the sand, their manes blowing in the wind. Bead necklaces, bracelets, anklets and headbands completed their look of urban refugees in an imaginary tribe of noble savages. There were no boom boxes on that mythical shore, only guitar playing and singing—*If you're going to San Francisco/be sure to wear some flowers in your hair.../If you come to San Francisco/Summertime will be a love-in there.* That was not Scott McKenzie, but it was good enough to fill the late morning atmosphere with languorous daydreaming. The smell of pot was heavy even in the open. The vastness of the ocean could not absorb it. But the cops rarely showed up, and when they did everybody made the two-finger peace sign—"Peace, man"— and moved a few yards away. There was no confrontation, no violence. At least, not there. Not yet.

Cindy and Ken were sitting in a group nearby. They shared the house with us and a few others. Cindy saw me and waved, signaling, *"Come and join us."* I waved back, *"Later. I want to go swimming."* Cindy shook her head, *"Bad idea."* She braced herself and shivered, *"The water is cold."* I gestured back, *"I don't mind."*

I got up and ran toward the waves, long waves rolling onto the beach with a splash of white foam. They were tall and powerful, and the impact was strong. One wave rolled me over. It was not a pleasant swim, it was a struggle with Nature, and the water was frigid, good for the seals that lived along the coast. Not for me. I am a creature of the Mediterranean, where the water near the coast is a primordial soup that soothes muscles and worries alike. Two minutes later, I ran back to my towel.

It was a bad idea, Cindy was right. Why did I do it? Not just to prove to myself that I was brave. I guess I did it to have an excuse not to join the group. I felt like I didn't belong with them. I didn't smoke, not even regular cigarettes. So, I couldn't simply sit in their circle and say no thanks I pass... Ridiculous.

Cindy came up to me. She was pretty, a fresh flower

blooming in her hair. Long, blond, straight, silky hair. The kind I liked. The kind I wished I had. But mine was short, wavy and light brown with golden highlights.

"Am I bothering you? If you'd rather be alone, just say so."

"On the contrary, I enjoy your company. Please, sit down." I was sincere. I truly liked her.

Cindy sat down on the edge of my towel. "You've got goose bumps. I warned you about the water."

"Yes, you did. But I've been here for only three months and there are many things I've got to get used to."

"Like what?"

"Like corn flakes for breakfast and square bread in plastic wraps. And especially the academic system, which is quite different from the one back home."

"Why aren't you at school today?"

"I've classes in the afternoon. I'll have to leave in a short while."

"And Jim?"

"What about him?"

"D'you have to get used to him as well?"

I was surprised Cindy would ask me such a personal question. But I was also pleased because I needed a friend, someone to talk to.

"I guess so," I replied, "things are not going smoothly between us."

"How did you two meet?"

"It's a long story. We met in Italy, during the campus occupation at the University of Turin, my hometown."

Trouble had just started. Those were the first signs, well before the Red Brigades came into existence and terrorized the country for more than a decade. The students had occupied the administration building, a stately Baroque palace in the heart of the city. A banner hanging from the façade said in big characters: UNIVERSITÀ OCCUPATA. The massive portals were closed and guarded by militant fellows with red armbands. They would let in, by a small door, only those who could show the proper credentials. A large number of students crowded the portico in front of the building and spilled out into the street, blocking the traffic in both directions.

I was in the crowd with my boyfriend, Giorgio, mainly to find out what was going on. We didn't belong to any radical movements and hardly knew what their demands were. An animated discussion was taking place right in that spot. A student in a Che Guevara beret was haranguing those who gathered around him:

"No more grades based on an unjust evaluating system. We demand political grades for all. Equality of grading."

"What's a political grade?" someone asked.

"We maintain that you should be evaluated not on the basis of false knowledge inculcated on the masses by the hegemonic professorial class, but on the basis of your belief in the cause and your involvement in the struggle."

"I agree, school must be radically reformed," another said.

"No, not reformed. It should be abolished. The whole bourgeois educational system must be overthrown," still another replied.

A guy a few years older, who did not seem to belong in that crowd, managed to make himself heard.

"We don't want to abolish the school. We want the right to go to school. I am a metal worker and represent the Union. Some of you guys asked me to come to this rally today to see whether we can make common cause. But the Union disagrees with your demands. I was not able to go to school. I had to go to work as a young boy. And I don't want my little brother to have to do the same. I want him to get an education."

"The working class has sold out to its masters," shouted the Che Guevara guy.

"This is a provocateur," said a student pointing a finger at the Union man.

A scuffle erupted, and the man would have been badly beaten if the police had not been on their way. At the sound of the approaching sirens, the crowd froze and then frantically tried to disperse. But the police had already surrounded the area.

Many were clubbed and many were arrested. A few managed to escape. Tear gas was rapidly filling up the street. Giorgio and I got separated. I was swept along the portico that extended for the entire length of the street by a stream of panicking students. All the stores were locked and looked empty. I stopped in the doorway to a bookstore to catch my breath, choking on the gas. I must have cut a rather pathetic figure. Suddenly, the door opened. A hand grabbed me by the arm and pulled me in.

"It looks like you can use some help," the guy said with a sly grin. He had a foreign accent—definitely, American.

"What makes you think so? I was just window shopping," I answered in the same vein, freeing my arm. I hurriedly wiped my tearing eyes. As my sight cleared, I took a good look at him. He was handsome, longish blond hair, a square jaw, blue eyes sparkling with a roguish smile.

"If you're interested in books, this is the place. I spend the good part of my days in here and always find what I look for."

"And what're you looking for?" I asked staring at him intently.

"You mean, other than books?" He held my stare and for a second we weighed each other up. Then, we both laughed.

He extended his hand, "I'm Jim Welsh. Let me buy you a cup of coffee."

"Impossible. All cafés around here are closed."

"We don't have to go out. BarbaGian keeps a fresh pot of coffee in the back for the regulars all day long." Jim pointed to the old man behind the counter.

"Is this his name?" I suppressed a burst of laughter, looking alternately at the name written on the store window and the man with big round eyeglasses, his nose buried in a book.

"Why? Is it funny?"

"Yes. It means UncleJohn in the local dialect, but it's also the name of an owl species."

"Well, then it's quite appropriate for a book lover."

In the small lounge in the back, I learned that Jim was a Fulbright fellow with a PhD in film studies. He took one-year leave from the university where he taught as a lecturer to write a book that he believed would propel his career. The book explored how early Italian movies influenced Hollywood silent epics. That's why he learned Italian. He chose to do research in Turin because at the beginning of the century this was the movie capital of Italy. There were twenty-one film production companies in town, which competed with the Rome studios, and gained the upper hand abroad not only for artistic creativity, but also for their commercial and financial organization. It was in Turin that movies became an industry, and that a model for 'movie making' developed and was then adopted worldwide. Jim found a lot of valuable materials, texts and pictures, in BarbaGian's innermost vaults.

"I'm particularly interested in Giovanni Pastrone, producer, director and stage designer," he told me after BarbaGian brought us two steaming cups of coffee and a tray of patisserie. "In his masterpiece *Cabiria*, which came out in 1914, beside the superb scenography of the temple of Moloch, he introduced special effects to represent the eruption of Mount Etna, brought live elephants to the Alps to shoot the scene of the descent of Hannibal's army into Italy, and created an enormous faceted hexagonal mirror for the Sicilian episode in which Archimedes sets fire to the Roman fleet."

"Is it true that Griffith's set for the Babylon episode of *Intolerance* displays architectural features similar to *Cabiria*'s?"

"No one can deny it. Just look at those frames side by side—the gigantic elephant-columns, just to name one. Pastrone was the inventor of the 'colossal,' with hundreds of extras and complex scenes of battles and catastrophes. He was not content with small scale models. For *The Fall of Troy* he had an enormous wooden horse built from scratch." Jim became more and more animated as he talked. It was obvious that he identified with Pastrone's creative genius.

"Your book won't be popular in Hollywood," I teased him.

"Perhaps. In any case, it'll stir some controversy. I'm ready to debate anyone. And there's more. Pastrone was a great innovator. He invented the 'tracking shot,' which forever changed the way to make movies. Now, the camera moves, it's a dynamic agent that adds points of view and emotions to the story."

"I didn't know Pastrone held that distinction."

"Yes, he did. But Hollywood was interested in Pastrone not just for his shooting techniques. Pastrone ran his studio, Itala Film, as an industry; to the production division he added a distribution network and a chain of movie theaters. It's not excluded that the Italian model inspired the 'integrated vertical structure' of the Hollywood studios."

"You're going to challenge the status quo."

"That's my intention."

"But with hundreds of controversial topics to choose from, why did you make this particular director the focus of your research?"

"I admire creativity. Besides, this is such an interesting piece of history. And, possibly, a good editorial scoop."

In the weeks and months that followed, I spent long hours at BarbaGian's, browsing the stacks, leafing through dusty manuscripts, going through original editions of scripts and scenarios, reading reviews and opinions on the cultural pages of old newspapers collected by year and tied together with a string, and copying by hand all the excerpts we considered relevant (this was before the Xerox machine). I neglected my own studies in order to spend the days with Jim.

In the stacks, he would suddenly approach me from behind, put his arms around me pressing his body against mine, seek my neck with his lips, and move slowly upward toward the ear. His tongue would swirl around with a slow movement tracing every bend and nook inside that live seashell, triggering electric waves that traveled down the spine and died there with a spasm of desire.

After work, we would stop at a *trattoria* on our way to Jim's place. The *trattoria* was popular with the students living off campus. Two waiters with napkins hanging from their left arms ran back and forth among the tables in the smoke-filled room, carrying large trays overloaded with orders—minestrone, polenta with beef stew, and onion frittata, simple dishes at an affordable price. The owner would seat the guests and make sure there was a bottle of house wine on every table.

One evening, the militant group I saw at the rally was dining in a corner behind a partition. Their loud voices filled the whole place—slogans, declarations, rebuttals.

Jim tilted his head in their direction. "Your comrades're having a cell meeting tonight."

"*My* comrades? I don't even know them."

"They're idiots."

"Pard'me...?"

"Yes, idiots. They are caricatures of those who in the course of history have believed in a noble cause."

"Perhaps they have a point, our society is stagnant and corrupt..."

"Idiots don't have a point. They're dangerous. They can cause a lot of trouble."

"You don't understand because you're American."

"And what's that supposed to mean? That we Americans are dumb when it comes to understanding the great sophistication of the European mindset? I have a PhD and two Masters, one in history and one in philosophy. I did my homework, and I know what I'm talking about. Besides, we have our share of idiots as well. But those are different, the opposite of your militant activists. Those are 'gentle people' who want to change the world through 'flower power.'"

"Here there's a lot of admiration for Martin Luther King and his struggle for civil rights."

"Who's the one that does not understand now? You're comparing apples and oranges. Dr. King's a great leader, an enlightened mind, and a true transformational figure who has achieved the unthinkable. He had the courage to challenge an unjust system with the sheer strength of his convictions. And now, the Civil Rights Act is law. But he worked hard for that and continues to do so. You won't see him hanging out in Haight-Ashbury smoking pot and weaving flower wreaths."

"There may be a difference in style, but in the end it all boils down to love." I resorted to the proven slogan that was supposed to win the argument and close the case.

Dinner was over. The waiter brought us two shots of grappa. Jim dipped a finger in his glass and touched my lips.

"*This* is love," he said.

I sucked his finger with relish.

Our eyes locked.

"Let's go home, darling," Jim said in a deep voice. He took me by the hand and led me to the door.

That night, like every night, while we walked the few blocks to Jim's apartment, the world gradually lost its contours. Like through a zoom lens, my vision was funneled toward a focal point that became larger and larger as we reached our destination, while the peripheral field faded out—the street, the building, the apartment, the bed, we in bed, we together, we becoming one. Our intertwined bodies were the fusion point which included the whole universe.

Words were not necessary. Jim knew how to talk to me with his hands, his kisses, his entire body, in a seductive language that made me follow his lead. And the surrender was sweet. Sweet and intense and desperate, because I knew the end would come soon.

Jim rented a small apartment in a stately building on the bank of the Po River, on the top floor. Practically it was a garret under the roof, but the view from the dormer was splendid. To reach the dormer one had to climb two steps, and from there the eye would soar and dance in the sky like a kite, taking in the details of the landscape, starting with the red tiles on the roof, moving down to the yellow-green strip of the river that looked absolutely still from that distance, encased in granite walls softened by a line of sycamore trees, a brush stroke of new green foliage, and beyond the trees, the dark-green slopes of the hills that bordered the city from the south-west. On the other side of the hills was Villa Flora, and further on in that direction was the sea, and then the ocean, and on the other shore, America.

Another month and Jim would be gone. I could not stand the thought of it. That's why, when he asked, I agreed to go with him.

It was not that simple, though, and if it were not for Amy I may have probably decided otherwise. Amy had been my closest friend since we were children, always pushing me to be bold, to love the adventure, to follow the heart. We debated this issue back and forth. "I would have to interrupt my studies just one year before graduation," I'd say. "But you can enroll in graduate school over there. They'll give you credit for the work you've already done here." "What if I won't succeed?" "You will succeed. We've already decided to go to grad school in the States. Dad has agreed to arrange for everything when the time comes. He lives over there and knows what to do. So, what's the difference?" "The difference is that if I leave now I'll be on my own. He won't help. This is scary." "C'mon, Stella. Don't be a child." "And then, there's Giorgio. He loves me, and I don't want to hurt him." "He'll find himself another girl and forget about you." "Oh, that's painful." "But you love Jim, don't you?" "Yes, I do,"

Mother did not try to stop me, although she was worried about this reckless adventure. One thing is to go to graduate school with a solid degree already under your belt—she'd caution me—and be accepted in advance by the university of your choice. But just to follow a man to a place you didn't choose, and then apply when you're there, and leave everything to chance... it's not wise. And besides, Jim is not reliable. He's charming, I give you that, and has a Romantic aura around him... I understand the way you feel. And I also realize that professionally you'll have better opportunities over there. So, I will not discourage you. But be prepared to face reality. You'll have to make it on your own with no help from anyone.

I would reply that I'd give myself six months, and if I see that I cannot make it, that I'm not strong enough, then I'll come back. But she would disapprove of this plan as well, saying that this would be a cop out. Choices have consequences, and one should face those consequences responsibly. At that point, I knew that she expected me to be brave, strong and successful, and that to come back in defeat would have been too great a humiliation for me.

"Wow, what a story! You should try and sell it to a Hollywood producer. They like love stories with a happy ending," Cindy said.

"Well, this is only the end of Part One. Now Part Two has started, and the ending's not necessarily going to be a happy ending."

"Oh, what a pity. D'you still love him?"

"Of course, I love him. But I'm not sure I like him these days. He's changed. He's depressed, unsociable, and angry all the time. Even at me."

"He must be unhappy."

"Yes, he is unhappy. But it's not my fault. He's unhappy because his book project has not been well received in the academic community. He's not got the expected endorsements from the senior faculty, and therefore two university presses have already rejected the proposal."

"So sorry. But I've got positive vibes about the two of you, and I'm sure everything will work out beautifully in the end."

"Thank you for the rosy forecast. Time for me to go. I've classes in an hour and I can't afford to be depressed. I must be super-efficient."

I picked up my towel and started back toward the cottage. Cindy stood there for a minute, a concerned smile in her eyes. She waved me good-bye, "Take it easy!" she yelled after me. I turned around and waved back.

Twelve o' clock. I had to quickly change clothes and be on my way. Jim was still asleep. I raised the venetian blinds with a sharp pull. A beam of light burst into the room like a punch. It hit him full-on.

"Whadda fuck you doing?" he muttered angrily, raising his head.

"Come on, Jim, get up. I'll fix you some lunch."

He turned to the wall, making disgruntled sounds, something unintelligible, "… and shut the goddam blinds," he concluded. That, I distinctly heard.

"Shut 'em yourself," I snapped back.

I slammed the door and was gone.

Stella's Story: Chapter 2
LA 1967

On the freeway I had the time to collect my thoughts and cool down. Because of the traffic, it would take me a good half an hour to reach the campus. I was driving an old Ford. Old, but still working and looking smart. I bought it from a used-car dealer for a ridiculously low price. Used-car dealers have a bad reputation here, they have been stereotyped as the ultimate conmen. But this one, when he learned that I was from Italy, became very friendly and said that his grandfather was Italian and, therefore, he wanted to help a *paisà*. I was lucky. The savings I brought from home had to last me a long time, and I had to be careful about spending money. With Jim we had agreed to split everything fifty-fifty—housing, food and all the other common expenses. He had a teaching job but his salary was at the bottom of the scale.

Six lanes of cars moved side by side like on a conveyor belt, all at the same speed. The pace, however, was sustained. I started maneuvering to move to the right lane in order not to miss my exit. Miraculously, everyone behind me slowed down and let me get across. They even smiled and signaled me to go. Courtesy. Simple, decent, civil behavior… This struck me from the very first day, because in Italy courtesy among strangers is a rare occurrence. Bad manners are the norm among people in the Old World. For example, in a similar situation, the drivers would start honking and accelerating, preventing me from moving across the lanes, and signaling with vulgar gestures that I'd better not get in their way.

Once, I told Jim how much I appreciated the courteous behavior I found here. "This is still the Wild West like you see it in the movies," he said. "In the frontier days, rude behavior would promptly get you a bullet in the head. So, people made sure to be very polite to each other, while keeping the finger on the trigger. Nothing really changed." Perhaps he was right. But even so, courtesy prevailed and that was very refreshing.

I left the car in a large parking lot on the outskirts of campus and walked briskly through the beautiful grounds, along manicured flower beds, emerald lawn and perfectly shaped trees. I didn't want to be late because my position was still rather shaky. I had applied for the PhD program in Comparative Literature, and I was given permission to attend classes as an auditor while the administration evaluated my records. If the decision were positive, I would be admitted to the program in January.

At the entrance, a black guy that seemed to be directing the traffic asked, "Did you come for the meeting? This way." He pointed to a large classroom full of people.

"Actually, I…don't know…"

"Move, quick. They've already started."

I found myself in the crowded room. A man and a woman sitting at a table conducted the meeting. They each sported a bushy Afro hairdo in the latest fashion. A banner on the wall behind them said *Black Students Union*. The audience was mixed, blacks and whites in equal numbers. The man at the table was speaking:

"…that's why we can't call a strike right now. Our goal's to close down this motherfucker and keep everyone out. But we've gotta have consensus. We've got no white support on this campus yet."

"Hey, man, there's a lot of white students already fighting the pigs out in the street," retorted a white guy from the audience.

"Don't gimme the same old jive. You shitheads get busted fo' grass and see yourselves as martyrs fo' the cause. But when you live in a ghetto, can't get a job, can't get food, and the fucking pigs keep busting your ass all the time, that's what makes you a revolutionary."

The woman sitting next to him took the floor, "The brother here's right. You white radicals are full of bullshit. You don't feel we have a common cause. But wait. If you do nothing to prevent it, we'll all be in the same bag. The pigs are already running amok. Soon they'll be all over campus, snooping around in the classrooms, the dorms, everywhere. This country's turning into a police state. D'you wanna wait till then to join the revolution?"

This is *déjà vu*, I thought to myself. They reminded me of the militant groups back in Italy. Another face of the rebellion. Nothing to do with the happy hippies on the beach.

"What you're saying makes sense, but the Strike Committee should also add some of our demands, you know, the NOW issues," voiced a female student.

"And also, let's end ROTC and the Vietnam War. It's now clear they're going to reinstate the draft. We can't allow that," added another guy.

"Well said, man," said the BSU leader. "You wanna end the fucking war, then get off your ass. Fill a bottle full of gasoline and go down to the ROTC office. Let 'em have a taste of your special cocktail."

"Yeah!" "Right on!" many among the blacks shouted from the floor.

I was near the door and I snuck out.

In the hall, I crossed Professor Worthington on his way out. I was surprised to see him because he was supposed to be in class.

"I apologize for being late," I said. "I hope you will allow me to attend the last hour."

"Don't worry," he answered, and there was a note of sadness in his voice, "the class has been cancelled. Political meetings, you know, strike committees, organizational rallies all over campus. Students don't go to class anymore... Unless you're Herbert Marcuse, of course. To his classes, they flock. Many have moved to San Diego to be where he is... Well, take care."

He got going toward the exit.

"Professor!" He stopped. "Can you give me some extra work until classes resume? Some readings I can do on my own?"

He looked at me with interest and curiosity. He was pushing seventy but his stare still had the spark of youth. A full head of white hair further brightened his handsome features. And he stood tall and straight. Must have been an athlete in his youth. His academic field was philosophy, in particular the Enlightenment and its heritage over the past two centuries.

"Are you sure you want to take some time off the 'revolutionary' activities?" he teased me.

"This is not really my thing, you know..." I assured him.

He kept staring at me for a few seconds, as if to convince himself that I was for real, and then extended me an invitation.

"In this case, why don't you come over for tea one of these days? My wife will be happy to meet you. And we will discuss this matter at ease."

I wanted to jump up and down, but I refrained and simply thanked him. Worthington had a lot of clout with the administration, and a word from him could really improve my chances.

To fill the rest of the time, I spent a few hours at the library. It was such a pleasure to be allowed to roam the stacks and pick up books from the shelves at will. Another big score for America. A rational and democratic library system. Yes, democratic, because the books were there for the users, and not for the institution. Compare it to Italy, where the institution is considered a sacred repository of knowledge and feels proprietary of its holdings. It keeps them under lock. In order to obtain a book, one must file a request and wait for a couple of hours, or a couple of days, depending on the circumstances and the mood of the library clerk. For me the American system was extraordinary, while for everybody else it was quite ordinary, it was simply the 'American way.' However, something was changing. The 'American way' was under attack from its disaffected children. Through their cultural revolution, the young aimed to rebuild the system according to new ideals, not realizing that those 'new ideals' were merely old stuff, stale borrowings from the Old World.

When I got home everyone was already sitting at the dinner table. I took my seat and apologized for being late. Nobody seemed to care, or to have noticed that I was missing. Only Cindy from the other end of the table sent me a big smile and a silent greeting. Loud talk and laughter went on without interruption. Those were the unwritten rules of our small community. The women would take turns and make dinner (yes, women only), and everyone was free to sit at the table to share in the food and the conversation, or equally free not to share, and his or her absence would be deliberately ignored. At first, I mistook this attitude for cold indifference, and even hostility. Only much later, I realized that it was just out of respect for people's privacy.

Hamlet got up and put a paw on my lap. I patted him on the head, wondering whether he was being friendly or was just hungry.

"Pass the meatloaf, would you?" I asked Kevin, who sat next to me.

Kevin was the latest addition to the household. He was an artist who dreamed of placing his works in top galleries, and for the moment worked as a freelance illustrator for a minor studio producing animation films for commercials. He was black, tall and handsome. Ken and Cindy brought him to home one day after meeting him on the street selling his paintings. Kevin had just arrived in LA from New York and was looking for a place to stay. There were no rooms available in the cottage. So, he settled in the shack in the backyard, which was large enough to accommodate his artwork.

The meatloaf was sent my way, followed by ketchup, mashed potatoes, and salad. I helped myself and put a little bit of everything on my plate. By now, I had learned that one was expected to pile up whatever food was on the table all together on a single plate. That's why the dishes were so large, much larger than the standard European dishes. The first time I had that experience I thought it was a barbaric practice that killed the pleasure of eating. Food was supposed to be savored in small quantities and in separate courses brought to the table in sequence, not to be swallowed down as a heap of mixed textures and flavors. But I got used to it, and even began to appreciate its practical side: fewer dishes to wash, which was important considering that this was a women's chore and there was no dishwasher in our primitive kitchen.

Jim was deeply involved in a discussion with Doug, and did not even say hello. Perhaps he was still mad at me for our morning fight. Or, he was embarrassed by it. Or, he was sorry but did not know how to say it... Whatever. I just ignored him.

"Look, man, if you want to advance in academia you've got to play the game," Doug was telling him.

"You've got to be a bootlicker. Is that what you're saying?"

"Come on, don't put it that way. You're pissed because Crafton doesn't want to endorse your manuscript. But he's not a bad guy. Can't you just suck up to him a bit?"

"Hell, no."

"But, look, he's the department chair and has to cover his ass. Besides, he gave you some suggestions for revisions that you ignored."

Doug was a colleague of Jim's, a few years older. He was still a junior faculty but had a tenure-track position—which means he knew how to play the game. His wife, Carol, was sitting directly across from me by their two kids, four- and five-year-old Linda and Ricky. The kids were engaged in painting a mustache on each other's face with ketchup. Carol snatched the ketchup bottle from their hands and whisked them to the bathroom for a scrub.

"I'm telling you, man, don't believe anything they say. They're just there to screw you," Kevin said, addressing no one in particular.

"Who're you talking about?" asked Doug.

"The establishment, man. An independent artist doesn't have a chance. No matter how good. Even Michelangelo had to kiss the pope's ass."

"Yeah, literally I bet." Jim's scurrilous comment made everybody laugh, including Kevin.

Kevin was not an angry man. He just played the role of the angry artist to entertain the audience. When he first showed me his work, he said he came from a middle-class family and attended classes at the Art Students League. "You see," he told me, "I used to paint the same shit as those guys in New York—Pollock and company. Brilliant artists, don't get me wrong. For some time I hung out with them. But I'm black, and now I'm searching for my roots and my ethnic form of expression. That's why I moved to California, far away from everything, to start anew on my own." I noticed that his latest canvases, still in the vein of Abstract Expressionism, displayed vibrant colors and shapes that evoked African jungles and deserts.

At the end of the table, Jack ate in silence. Most of the time he was deeply immersed in thought and estranged from the general conversation. However, after the latest comment on the establishment, he jumped in.

"This is no laughing matter. What we need is a full-fledged

revolution. A complete overturn of the fucking system. The total transformation of the country."

His tone was sharp and dogmatic, his eyes deep-set and intense, burning like coals on a pale face framed by straight black hair. He was a graduate student in political science and a member of the most radical Marxist group on campus.

There was no reply. Nobody wanted to engage in a discussion that would last forever and lead to nowhere.

We moved to the living room, each with a mug of coffee. Carol stayed behind to do the dishes. "Thanks for dinner," the guys told her politely, and gave her a peck on the cheek. She smiled and seemed to be pleased with their attentions.

I always felt uncomfortable on such occasions. Most women in those days seemed to accept without questioning the role that society expected from them. A secondary role. Betty Friedan had already published *The Feminine Mystique* and the NOW movement had just been born, but there was no widespread awareness of women's rights yet. Once, I brought it up with Carol, "Why is it that even in a fringe household like ours women have a well-defined role, that of homemakers? This seems to be the norm for all couples, married and unmarried." "Not really, I see a real change taking place. The sex revolution is changing traditional society, and alternative life styles are being adopted by a large number of young people." "Yes, but the woman in the couple still has a subordinate position. And she doesn't challenge it, her consciousness is still dormant." "Well, I don't mind doing things for Doug, you know. He's happy if I cook a good meal and take care of his clothes and keep the house clean... He really appreciates it." "I bet he does. Anyway, this is a big surprise for me. We from Europe regard the States as being a progressive country. And yet, even in Italy women are more aware of their rights as a person." "What d'you mean?" "I'm not saying that Italian women are emancipated and have equal rights... Far from it. They were not even allowed to vote until the mid-forties, and still there's no divorce law. Cases of victimized and abused housewives are frequent and brutal, and when dealing with murder often the law sides with the husband on the ground that he acted to defend his 'honor.' The difference is that women in Italy are quite resentful of their lower status, and do not accept their role lightly. Resentment is brewing, and it's tangible in their relationship with men. Here you do the dishes with a smile, there they do the dishes with a grudge."

"Well, for many women the smile may be a mask."

Jack retreated to his room soon after dinner. He never socialized. Kevin sat on the couch with Ken and Cindy to share a joint. Doug and Jim lit up regular cigarettes. Jim didn't want to 'fuck up' his system with drugs, as he put it, but at the same time he went through two packs of Benson & Hedges a day. I was constantly shrouded in a cloud of smoke, and totally oblivious of its effect. It didn't bother me. Probably because I grew up in a smoking society and had absorbed the poison since childhood. And yet, I did not smoke. I tried it once and didn't like it. The fact that I was not a smoker was seen as an eccentricity in our community, sort of a snobbish attitude that further set me apart from the rest.

Doug turned on the TV. A series of commercials tried to convince us that Coca-Cola is the real thing, Tide is the best detergent, Volkswagen makes the best cars, Kellogg's the best cereals, GE the best electric razors, Max Factor the sexiest lipstick... and each and all of these products would turn our lives around and make us the happiest people in the happiest of all possible consumer societies.

Then the news came up. Another bad day in Vietnam. More Americans killed. The footage showed our soldiers in the swamps with water up to their waist. Most were barechested because of the heat, and wore no helmet, just a bandana tied around the head or a foliage wreath as protection from the sun. They were sitting ducks for the invisible enemy to strike. Then there was a jump cut to helicopters bombing villages, and the commentator described it as President John-son's decisive response.

An image of campus unrest produced a different com-mentary, "*Hey hey LBJ / How many kids / You've killed today.*"

"Shit!" Doug said, "The guy's crazy. He keeps escalating and we keep losing our men by the thousands."

"Don't feel sorry for 'em. They support the war, an evil war. They volunteered. We want peace. Peace, man," Ken said, keeping his vacant eyes away from the screen and tak-ing a long drag on the joint Cindy handed him.

"You must be kidding, you jerk!" Jim jumped in. "Who volunteered? The poor devils who couldn't go to school, who didn't have a job, who needed a paycheck to support the fam-ily, those who were bamboozled by the ROTC recruiters—the GI bill, free education, a good career, benefits, pension—yes, if they came back alive, this is what nobody told them. These guys are cannon fodder in the hands of the politicians…You make me sick, you sit on your fat ass all day long gazing at your navel and don't understand shit of the tragic reality of this war."

Ken did not react, he was too high.

Cindy answered for him, "He didn't mean anything bad. He's a gentle guy who loves everyone." She kissed him on a bushy cheek, and rested her head on his shoulder. She was obviously protective of him.

"You're a lovely girl." Jim's tone suddenly mellowed out. "Ken's a lucky man." There was a note of tenderness in his voice. Also, a longing for affection, a need for empathy. Stripped of anger, he now sounded very vulnerable, like a child who'd been hurt.

I felt the urge to take him in my arms. A heavy knot weighed on my chest and was slowly moving up toward the throat. I wanted to cry, for him, for me, for us together and yet apart. I lowered my eyes and picked up a magazine. Jim had not spoken to me the whole evening, and now he was getting up and would likely leave the room without saying a word. He would go out and come back late at night, and I would pretend to be asleep.

Instead, he stopped by my chair. I kept my eyes on the magazine and held my breath. He took my hand and said gently, "Come, I want to show you something."

He led me to the back porch and made me sit on the steps. He put an arm around my shoulders and with the other indicated a point in the distance, "Look up there, beyond the fence," he said.

A tall eucalyptus cut a sharp figure against the dark sky. From our point of view, it stood alone, as if framed by the hand of an artist. In the moonlight, it twinkled with the silvery tremor of thousands of leaves, a myriad of sparks quivering in the breeze, a silent cluster of fireworks, a magic fountain of dreams.

"It's so beautiful…" I whispered with tears in my eyes.

"Yes, pure beauty." Jim held me tight, fighting to suppress an intense emotion. We remained like that for a long time, together.

The moonlight entered the room and caressed our bodies. On the bed, our bodies talked to each other in silence. They performed a love dance, intertwined, ancient movements forever renewed, ancestral memories in novel emotions, cosmic intuitions through flesh contact, melodic vibrations of organic waves, a sweet death in the spasm of pleasure.

"I feel great," Jim said afterward, and kissed me tenderly on a shoulder. He looked happy and relaxed. "What a fantastic fuck."

"What?! Is that all you can say?"

"Well, don't you agree?"

"Yes, but can't you say something sweeter?"

"I guess I can't. If I said 'I love you' or stuff like that it wouldn't sound right because I grew up without love. No-body said 'I love you' to me when I was a kid. So, now I can *act* on my feelings, but I can't *talk* about them. I'm sorry, it must be tough for you to live with someone like me."

"Yes, it's not easy. I don't believe in suffering, and I should not be the target of your anger. On more than one occasion I've been on the brink of leaving."

"Don't leave. I want you to stay." A plain, unadorned, un-sentimental statement that said it all and filled me with over-whelming joy. I made myself a niche against his body.

"Were you unhappy as a child?" I asked.

"Unhappy? I don't think I was. I became independent at a very early age. I learned to take care of myself and didn't need any pampering. Mother was not a sentimental type. She was extremely efficient, ran the household with clockwork preci-sion, and kept everything spick-and-span including the chil-dren. My brothers and I always had that scrubbed look, you know, freshly pressed clothes and a special barber haircut, tightly cropped hair all over with a moderate shock on the forehead. On Sundays, we went to church in suit and bowtie. It was a Southern Baptist church, and all the kids looked alike in the same proper attire."

"Did she kiss you good night when you went to bed?"

"At bedtime she was busy with my twin brothers, who were younger than I. When I was about four—before that I have no memories—she'd just shout out so that I could hear her from the living room, 'Jimmy, bedtime!', and I would rush to her, give her a peck on the cheek and go to my room. Then, in bed with my eyes shut I'd see her face radiating in the dark... A beautiful face, to which I was irresistibly attracted. But as I moved toward her, she seemed to retreat. And I'd play that game for a long time, till I fell asleep."

"You didn't have a nanny?"

"No, we didn't. We had a housekeeper during the day, a black woman who's still with the family after thirty years.

But at night she went home, she had her own family to take care of. Occasionally there were babysitters, when my parents went out. With them it was fun, I stayed up till late and we played games because back then there were no videos to watch."

"Were you close to your father?"

"That jerk? No, I hated him."

"That's a pretty strong word."

"Well, it'is the truth." Jim lit up a cigarette. "He was a fanatic disciplinarian. In those days, and until I left home at eighteen, his mission was to teach us respect and obedience. With my little brothers he was a bit more reasonable, but with me he was inflexible."

"For example…?"

"For example, one day I was riding my bicycle and one of the housekeeper's kids suddenly crossed my path. I tried to stop but I couldn't, and we crashed and fell to the ground. Nobody was hurt and we got up laughing about the accident. But father, who saw the scene, came out and dragged me inside, and lectured me for half an hour about the fact that I, because of my privileged position, had a responsibility toward those who were more vulnerable, especially the blacks. As a punishment, he forced me to give my bicycle to the kid, and didn't buy me a new one for a whole year… I think he was sick. Nowadays, the shrinks would call it a professional disease."

"What does it mean?"

"He was a defense lawyer, and one obsessed with the idea of justice. We lived in a segregated society, and racial problems were particularly severe in that area."

"You told me you're from the Deep South, but where from exactly?"

"A small town south of Atlanta. When I was a kid the old plantations were long gone but many blacks still worked in the cotton fields for a pittance. They were constantly harassed and thrown in jail under the slightest pretext, often on false charges. Father always took up those cases. But he didn't do it for humanitarian reasons. No. He did it because he placed the law above everything. I don't think he related to his clients as human beings, just as defendants with certain rights under the law. He was honest and principled to a fault, and for that he was considered an eccentric among his peers. But they respected him because he was a brilliant lawyer who never lost a case. He could have made a lot of money, but he didn't. His clients were poor people and often he defended them for free."

"I don't understand what this has to do with you."

"*What*, you say? Everything. Father was the descendant of plantation owners, and proud of it. The old manor house and the surrounding grounds in my days were a historical site and belonged to the county. The site was not far from where we lived, and we could see busloads of tourists arriving on weekends. He kept telling me that because of our heritage we were the leading class, and therefore had a responsibility toward society and must set the example. He held me up to an impossible standard and kept moving the bar higher and higher so that I could never clear the mark. He played a sadistic game with me."

"Are you sure you're not exaggerating?"

"Well, he'd certainly disagree with my view. But then, we disagreed on everything."

"I guess you didn't get his blessing when you moved to California."

"Hell, no. That was a big blow for him. He wanted me to become a lawyer, of course. Instead, as soon as I graduated from high school I left home and went to LA to pursue a career as an actor. Without a penny. I had to support myself doing menial jobs. The worst was the night shift pushing broom in a food-processing plant. Shit, that was hard. But eventually I put myself through college and grad school. I did some acting for a while, enough to lose my Southern accent. Then I found myself deeply involved in academic life—books, ideas, innovative projects… It was exciting, I felt I could really make a difference…"

"And what about your father?"

"He's dead now. Over the years we tried to patch things up. We had a civil relationship, but we never warmed up to each other." His tone stiffened. "One thing is sure, I'll never have kids of my own. I don't want to be as bad a father as he was."

"But you're getting along so well with Linda and Ricky. You seem to have a good time with them."

"They're funny. It's like watching a Tom and Jerry cartoon. And the best thing about it is that, like a cartoon, I can turn it off and walk away when I'm tired. They're not my kids."

"I'm sure you'll change your mind. Perhaps, you need help…"

"Look, I don't want to change. And I don't need your sympathy. Save your bleeding heart for a better cause."

His good mood was gone. The tone was sharp. His attitude, hostile. I did not see it coming. I should have been more cautious, more discreet… But now it was too late.

He pushed me away. "Move over, go to sleep. I want to read for a while."

He turned on the nightlight, lit up another cigarette, and took a book from a pile he kept by the bedside.

He was lost to me, as far away as on another planet.

Two hours later, he turned off the light and plunged into a deep sleep. But I could not sleep, and went through the night with a thorn in my heart, trying to understand whether I felt guilty or hurt.

Stella's Story: Chapter 3
LA 1968

The winding road to Professor Worthington's house unfolded leisurely up the Bel Air hills. The mansions on both sides, hardly visible behind tall fences and luxuriant gardens, spoke of old money. Worthington himself came from a family who made its fortune in real estate in the booming twenties.

The gate was wide open and I turned onto a driveway paved with red bricks. It was winter, but plants still in bloom and evergreens created the illusion of a perennial spring. The driveway was lined with laurel trees. Their pungent fragrance blended with the scent of ferns, shrubs, and vines scattered on the vast grounds in carefully studied disorder. That sensual bouquet made me keenly aware of the peculiar atmosphere of that place. It was a place at once ancient and new, like the gigantic oak tree which stood sixty foot tall on the front lawn, where it had been standing for two-hundred years, when there was no house but only forest, and which greeted every spring with a fresh coat of green.

As I cleared the last rows of the verbena edge, I saw the house. It was a large three-story house in Spanish Revival style with some Baroque elements that marked the 'eclectic' trend of the early 1900s. The overall impression was of elegance and simplicity: textured white stucco walls, square angles, and a wing that stood taller than the main body, a sort of turret with an arcaded terrace under the red tile roof. But the doorway was decorated with an elaborate terracotta frame and two twisted columns, and featured a carved walnut door—an eccentric touch the master architect added as a flourish to his signature.

A maid opened the door and said that Professor and Mrs. Worthington were expecting me. She led me through several halls to the back portico, and left. The portico ran the whole length of the house, with a succession of tall arches closed at the base by wrought iron railings. The central arch did not have a railing, and from there red brick steps led to the garden. Outdoor chairs and couches, softened by puffy cushions in pastel colors, dotted the large veranda. From there, one could enjoy the view of a cobalt blue swimming pool surrounded by thick vegetation.

"Hello, darling. I'm so glad to meet you. Lee will be here in a minute. And, by the way, you can call me Marjorie. I don't stand on ceremony. Please, sit down."

I greeted the woman, and we sat down on a couch the same pale aqua color as her dress. Marjorie was the perfect complement to the house. In her early sixties, she had maintained a fresh look, a slender figure, and a radiant smile. She later told me, proudly, that those were *her own* teeth. Her gray hair, cut short, had a youthful shine. She wore a silk chemise dress with flat sandals and a coral necklace.

"It's a long drive up here. Have some mango juice while we wait for Jeannette to bring tea."

She handed me the glass. I complimented her for the house.

"Thank you. I adore it. We've been living here for forty years, and never for a minute had I wished I lived somewhere else, although we've been all over the world... I'll tell you about it someday. But now, I want to know more about you. Are you married? Are you happy here?"

"I'm okay. But there are some problems I must solve."

"You just said something very true: 'problems *I* must solve.' Don't you ever forget that. You're in charge of your life. Friends may help, but you're the boss. Your happiness depends on you."

There was genuine empathy in her voice and a thought crossed my mind, *I found a friend.* Or, perhaps it was not a thought, it was a feeling, refreshing and soothing like the mango juice I had just swallowed.

Lee came in from the garden, running up the steps after the dog. Polo shirt, slacks, loafers, he looked like one of his students against the glowing light of the late afternoon.

"I see you two have already met. Pard'me for being late."

"Hi, honey. We were doing just fine," said Marjorie. "We could've used a few more minutes, or the whole afternoon for that matter."

"Really, I'm sorry. Monty took me for a walk in the woods. He's the boss, I just follow him. I told him I had an appointment, but he refused to take me back in time."

Monty was now greeting me, sniffing at my legs and feet. I stroked his silky coat. A gorgeous golden retriever coat.

"What kind of a name is Monty?" I asked.

"It's short for Montesquieu. When we got him, I was writing a book on the French philosopher, and I thought the name would rub off on him and stimulate his brain. It worked, now he's the brightest in the family."

"Wait a minute! Speak for yourself," said Marjorie. She got up as Jeannette came in carrying a large tray. "Here's your tea. I'm leaving you two scholars to your erudite endeavors." Then she turned to me, "We'll get together soon and have some fun. Come, Monty, let's go."

They walked back to the house together, the woman and the dog, with the same elegant gait.

"Cream or lemon?" Lee asked.

"Just plain, thanks."

I had my hands around the steaming cup, breathing in the spiced aroma and waiting for him to speak.

He poured himself a whiskey and soda from a nearby table, then sat down on the couch across from me and lit up a cigarette.

"So, tell me what your goals are. What d'you want to achieve?"

"In the immediate future, I want to get admission to the PhD program."

"No, I mean in life. D'you have a dream?"

"Yes, I want to become rich and famous as a writer. But just for a start I would settle for a position as a college professor..."

He laughed. "Careful, I may resent your being so condescending."

"Oh, no no, I didn't mean to say anything disparaging. I have a great admiration for you. I read your books... Well, it just didn't come out right, I'm sorry."

He paused and looked at me, squinting his eyes through a puff of smoke.

"D'you know why I like you? Because you strike me as a genuine person. Someone who's independent-minded. That's refreshing when the trend among young people is to conform to a model, to adopt an ideology... Or, perhaps this is too big a word. Today's groups don't have an ideology, all they have are a few borrowed ideas. These kids fill up their mouths with words such as Marxism, Communism, class struggle, revolution, but they don't even know their true meaning. They lack historical knowledge, never went to the roots."

"That's what your classes are for, to teach the students the history of ideas."

"Yes, and you and a few others want to learn. But for the most part the students are not interested in what a coterie of wise guys back in France was thinking two hundred years ago, why those thinkers are still relevant today, how their ideas reached these shores and found their way into the fabric of our Constitution..."

"When you mentioned Montesquieu, I immediately

thought of his influence on James Madison and the other American founders."

"Exactly. That's where the principle of the separation of powers comes from. And not only. Although Montesquieu remained a monarchist, he was a champion of liberty, and formulated a clear definition of a modern 'republic,' as opposed to 'despotism.' But, how d'you know these things?"

"This is part of the humanistic curriculum in Italy. We have philosophy classes in high school, I mean, in the lyceum."

"Well, then you understand what I mean when I talk about conformism, losing individuality and becoming the 'mass.' This is one of the favorite words in Marxist parlance because the mass can be easily manipulated. All you need is a charismatic leader, a simplistic doctrine, smart images on posters and banners, and *le jeu est fait*, a new dogma is born, an absolute truth, and all genuflect to it. What's interesting is that in a society like ours this process can be very subtle. I'm not worried that today's 'revolutionaries' may overthrow the government. That's nonsense. But they are nevertheless a threat to our institutions in the long run."

I helped myself to more tea.

"Much of it is a provocation—the way they dress, behave, speak, their songs, their slogans, their icons. But some of their demands make sense, don't you think? For example, protesting the war. And in general, it seems to me that all nations need a sort of renewal once in a while, a shock wave that would jolt them into a new phase of progress."

"You have an idealistic view of things, very Hegelian. Unfortunately, history teaches us that the dialectics of progress often doesn't work as postulated. What comes after the 'jolt' may turn out to be a regression. Most revolutions consolidate into a totalitarian state."

"Not the American Revolution..."

"Oh, that's different. Those revolutionaries didn't seek to seize power and occupy Buckingham Palace. Rather, they claimed the right to the territory that they had inhabited and developed for about two centuries. It was a war of independence rather than a revolutionary war. And the result was magnificent. True, there were things they didn't fix, like slavery for example. But, you see, a nation, like a person, matures over time, it acquires a higher consciousness, and things that look abhorrent to us today may have seemed necessary then. This may sound like a paradox, but the founding fathers, while believing in lofty humanitarian ideals, were also pragmatists. They had a job to do. The economic reality could not be ignored. I suppose the issue of slavery was simply put on the back burner. Nevertheless, it was precisely those principles they wrote in the Declaration of Independence that later on made abolition inevitable. Those were tough-minded guys, and they founded an exceptional nation."

"Exceptional… Well, yes I agree, but today's cultural revolution seems to challenge the concept of 'exceptionalism'."

"No doubt. Look, this generation is terribly disappointed with our intervention in Vietnam. And I cannot blame them. It turned out to be a great mistake. No person in good conscience can still support this destructive policy. But we have legal means to dissent with the government and to correct our mistakes without destroying our beliefs. 'We the people' *are* the nation, not the government. It's up to us. 'Exceptionalism' is part of the epic that brings us together and nurtures our pride as citizens. We must keep it alive."

"Some argue that it's the same as nationalism."

"No way. Just the opposite. This country is 'exceptional' because in the history of mankind no other country had ever been founded on the idea of government *by* the people—with the addition, of course, of *of* and *for*—which means people seen as citizens with an inalienable right to be equal and free. As citizens, not as subjects of the powers. This was the 'exception' from the norm. Therefore, we are right to say that the United States is different from all other nations and that we're proud to be citizens of this great country we created. Conversely, a nationalist discourse, like in Nazi Germany for example, would go like, 'Our country is the greatest in the world because we are a superior race, and therefore we feel free to go and occupy other countries in order to expand our supremacy.' Do you see the difference? The foreign policy of the United States seeks to build alliances and cooperation, while acting in the national interest. I must admit that at times things may go wrong. We are a superpower after all, and it's easy to cross that fine line between mutual advantage and imposing our values on others. When it happens, it's unfortunate. We should be careful never to lose sight of our fundamental principles."

"In Italy, the United States was much loved for its role in World War II. But now, with most youth being leftist sympathizers, or even militant activists, that sentiment has changed. They see the U.S. as an imperialistic power."

Lee took a long draw on his cigarette and paused. He seemed to concentrate on his thoughts.

"I fought in that war," he said gravely. "I was an Army major, among those who opened the gates to the concentration camps. I saw what evil looks like. We defeated it on that occasion, but not permanently. It keeps coming back. I'm not a theologian and I'm not talking of evil in metaphysical terms, but as a human negative force that for a series of circumstances gets the upper hand."

"Is it on the rise again?"

"Unfortunately, yes. The current evil is Communism, another totalitarian ideology similar to Nazism, only of a different color. Recently, it has acquired geopolitical relevance as the ideology of our rival superpower. That's why we're engaged in the Cold War with the Soviet Union. Our engagement is important to keep their power in check. But this does not mean that we should go and police every commie state around the world. As the Vietnam fiasco teaches us, we are now seen as the bully attacking the little guy. Which is not who we are."

"I want to ask you… Why d'you think Marxism is so appealing to young people? I want to know because, I must confess, I too am attracted by its basic ideas of equality and brotherhood … the barricades and all that …"

"Why? Because they don't understand it. That's obvious. Equality and brotherhood are noble ideas. How can anyone be against them? But they get distorted and corrupted when a tyrannical system operates in the name of those same ideas in order to enslave the people. As I was saying, the mass is easy to manipulate. The people can be duped into thinking that the state works for them and takes care of their needs. While the truth is that the state's only interest is to consolidate its power and keep the population under control with the allure of entitlements, and when this is not enough, with brutish force."

I swallowed a big gulp of tea.

"Luckily, this will never happen here."

"Not if we defend our republic. Otherwise, today's 'revolution' will erode our values. Many of those who today get indoctrinated will eventually move up through the system and become the leaders of tomorrow, and so will their children. They'll control politics, education, the media, entertainment … Gradually the government will expand, encroaching on individual freedoms. Orwell set that scenario in *1984*."

"Yes, I read that novel. What a nightmare."

"In our country, I would give it some more time. But if we don't defend our values, in thirty… forty years, let's say into the new millennium, free enterprise will struggle to survive because of government regulations and taxation, the majority of the population will be poor because of high unemployment, and will rely on food stamps and other government subsidies, the nation will be deeply in debt because without economic growth revenues will dwindle, state security will have at their disposal new and powerful technology to keep an electronic eye on everyone and report to the authorities. And the leaders, with the complicity of the media, universities, and the entertainment industry, will convince the population to vote for them in rigged elections, in exchange for more handouts from the treasury coffers... Until, one day, the coffers will be empty."

"I cannot even imagine such a scenario. This is the strongest economy in the world..."

"It would not be the first superpower to crumble. Take the example of ancient Rome. The mores of the empire eroded the republican values. The government became corrupt and inept, the people complacent, satisfied with handouts from above, *'panem et circenses,'* 'bread and entertainment.' That's still how those in power appease the masses, today and in the future. They establish an entitlement society, dependent on government and grateful for it. And in the process they destroy the 'citizen,' they destroy civil society, the community of individuals who think and act independently, and whose combined will and labor sustain a healthy and thriving economy."

"D'you really think American society could one day be radically transformed?"

"It depends on us, and on how we react to a perceived power grab. Look, civil society is what defines us as Americans. Tocqueville recognized this immediately when he came to visit the States in the 1830s and wrote his lucid assessment of American democracy as something new and different from the systems in Europe. He pointed out that people in the New World had acquired a new dignity through creativity and labor exercised freely, had become enterprising and self-reliant and, yes... rich. Unlike in Europe, he observed, the acquisition of wealth was not seen as vulgar, but as honorable, and was not disjointed from the moral principle of the common good. This is what made America an economic superpower. "

"So, in your scenario even the United States can become corrupt and go bankrupt?!"

"I hope not. Probably our resilient pioneer spirit will once again prevail. But I'm extremely concerned with what happens on our campuses nowadays, because I can see possible long-term consequences."

That day I left with a lot of unresolved questions on my mind. Going downhill, I saw in the valley below the thousands of lights of the city which is not a city, the amorphous spread of neighborhoods that do not blend, the endless network of streets and boulevards that stretch to infinity, and the glaring freeways writhing in sensuous loops like voluptuous snakes.

What is the answer? I asked myself. Philosophy is useful in formulating questions, rather than providing answers. Reason can help us to live better, but it cannot reconcile the existential paradoxes that keep us wondering. One has to find the answer elsewhere, through poetic intuition perhaps. Like, for example, in a silvery eucalyptus. As a great writer once wrote, "Beauty will save the world."

Stella's Story: Chapter 4
Santa Barbara, 1968

"Have you got everything?" I asked.

"Yes."

"I mean the manuscript."

"Yes, yes. Close the trunk, I can't see a thing in the rear." Jim was at the wheel, impatient to hit the road. Or just impatient, that's the way he was.

I closed the trunk and sat down in the passenger seat.

We were going to Santa Barbara for the weekend to visit with Larry. Amy, as a child, used to tell me how much she missed her father, and how much fun it was to be with him. She kept returning over and over to the first summer she spent in the States, when Larry took her to Santa Barbara and she went surfing and horse riding for the first time in her life. Now, Larry came down from New York, where he ran a large publishing house, to sell his parents' mansion that had been empty for years. I thought this would be a good occasion to introduce Jim and ask Larry to take a look at his manuscript. Perhaps, it would be better suited for a trade press than for elitist university presses.

At first, Jim was reluctant. But I insisted. "What d'you have to lose?" "I can lose my reputation as a scholar." "But L&N is a first-class press, very prestigious." "Yes, but it's not academic prestige." "Well, let's not jump to conclusions. Larry may not even be interested in your proposal." "Oh, this surely makes me feel good…" "Darling, I love you. Does *this* make you feel good?" "It does." Jim took my hand and pressed it against his lips.

The scenic vista of Highway 1 opened wide on the left—sand dunes, rocks, cliffs, flat beaches, pine trees, occasional rows of houses, some convenience stores and diners, all embraced by the curved line of the ocean glimmering in the sun. On the right, the yellow walls of the canyons.

June first... Jim had just bought a new car, a shiny red Mustang Fastback. Even if it was short of the Jag of his dreams, he loved it. We had the windows down and let the wind rush through our hair. School was almost over and we were on a short break before exams.

Things had improved in those months. I was admitted to the PhD program —thanks in part to Worthington's support. Jim was teaching a new film class, which was cross-listed with various departments and reached a student enrollment of over one hundred. The class focused on the new wave of Italian directors such as Fellini, Antonioni, Visconti, Pasolini and others, whose provocative films found a resonance on the left-leaning campus. And Jim took advantage of his position to inject serious knowledge into a field that most considered as mere entertainment.

He became very popular. Especially among female students, who were swept away by the dark aura that surrounded him as a young controversial professor, and by his good looks. And he was not indifferent to that kind of attention. I was well aware of some fooling around with this or that suntanned California beauty. But, oddly enough, I wasn't jealous. I knew my value, and my value to him. The other women did not represent a threat. Actually, in a strange way, I felt sorry for them, because I knew they didn't have a chance. Well, they did, an occasional fling perhaps. But I knew they could not have him. There was a bond between us. "We're a team," Jim would say with his contagious grin, to reassure me, but mainly to reassure himself. "We're a team." Fist bump.

Even on a gorgeous day like this, Jim liked to engage me in intense discussion. I guess it was part of our "being a team."

"I want to teach the students that films can be more effective than bombs in bringing about change. Not the mindless flicks they see at the drive-in, but those meant to raise social and political awareness can really boost the brain into independent thinking."

"So does art in general. It's the role of the artist to shock the public out of complacency and to challenge the conventions, first of all the aesthetic conventions by creating new forms of expression. And then, through the new language, to convey a new perception of the world."

"Absolutely. You put it better than everybody else, including the likes of Barthes, Derrida & Co. How can you be so smart?"

"Oh, don't be silly."

"I'm serious. And I'm very lucky." He reached over and squeezed my hand. "Take a director like Pasolini. He wants to expose a system in Italy that is centuries old and corrupt, based on the power of the bourgeoisie and the Catholic Church. Here, in our country, it's entrenched bigotry that should be attacked, that self-righteous, narrow-minded attitude prevalent in small-town America, but also present in larger cities, which stifles the spirit of our nation. Now, we're seeing a new trend emerging. Some filmmakers in Hollywood are stirring the waters. That's where the battle should be fought, in the intellectual field and in forums of discussion, not in the streets. The goal is to preserve our values, not to destroy them."

"Beautiful! You should become a politician."

"Impossible. I hate crowds."

"By the way, I heard that Bob Kennedy is going to speak tomorrow outside the Courthouse in Santa Barbara. It will be his last speech before the primary. Let's go to the rally."

"Hum... I just said I hate crowds."

"Come on! Don't be difficult."

"Well, you'll have to convince me." He gave me an enticing look. "Come close."

I did, and put my arm around his shoulders.

"Give me a kiss. No, not on the cheek... on the neck... a hot kiss. Move around... all around the ear... Yes, like this."

His neck was slightly salty. His fresh, natural taste mingled with the wind from the ocean which ruffled his hair.

He put a hand on my thigh and turned slightly toward me, rubbing his cheek against mine.

"Baby, why don't we stop at the first motel?" he suggested.

The car behind us started honking. We realized we had slowed down considerably. Jim pulled onto the right lane. The car passed us, and abruptly cut into our way, applying the brakes and almost causing an accident. We could see there were four guys inside. One of them mooned us in the back window.

"Asshole!" Jim shouted sticking his head out.

The driver gave him the finger. Then, the car sped away and disappeared behind a curve with its gang of juveniles.

"Motherfucker! He's dangerous. I'll report him to the highway patrol... Have you taken down the tag?"

"No... I didn't. It happened so fast."

"Shit! Now we've lost them." Jim punched the windshield with all his strength. A black belt punch. The windshield cracked. A large long-legged spider appeared before our eyes, giving us a distorted and fragmented view of the road. He was mad. Mostly at himself, because *he* didn't take down the tag. But he made it sound as if he were mad at me. At least, that's how I felt.

Our magic moment had dissipated. We proceeded at full speed, in silence.

I turned on the radio.

They say we're young and we don't know
We won't find out until we grow

Well I don't know if all that's true
'Cause you got me, and baby I got you.
Babe
I got you babe
I got you babe…

"Turn off that shit."
I turned off the radio.
"What bothers you?" I asked.
"Nothing."
"Everything."
"Look. This trip was your idea. I'm not enjoying it."
"That's clear. Anyway, let's stop for a cup of coffee, something to eat…"
"No, better keep going and make it in one stretch."
"But I have to go to the bathroom."
He made a disgruntled sound to express his frustration and did not answer. But soon we saw the sign for a Sambo restaurant and he took the next exit.
"Go to the bathroom while I fill up. Jesus, I can't believe these prices… 36 cents a gallon for regular, and it keeps going up."
Not far away in the parking lot, I recognized the car that gave us a hard time on the road. The four guys were hanging out, beer cans in hand, relaxing before continuing on their journey. They, too, had spotted us and were making jokes laughing out loud. As I passed by, the one who seemed to be the head of the pack made a catcall loudly enough for Jim to hear it.
"Hey, gorgeous, why don't you switch cars? We'd all appreciate a good blow job."
I pretended I didn't hear.
Jim came up to him. The other guys closed in behind the chief, ready for a fight.
Jim's eyes projected a calm fury. He took a fierce karate stance.

"The lady's my wife," he said. "You motherfucker, you apologize to her, or I'll tear your head off with my bare hands."

The force emanating from him was tangible, even without contact.

The guy backed off. He signaled the others to stand down.

"Easy, man. Just kidding. I meant no disrespect. Sorry, ma'am."

"Alright. Now get your ass out of here."

A minute later the car had disappeared.

"You've been magnificent," I told him. "Your karate training paid off big time."

"I didn't do it to show off my black belt."

"Why did you do it?"

He hugged me and held me tight.

"Because I love you," he said hiding his face in my hair.

We stood still in that position for a long time, in the middle of the parking lot. Our hearts beating together in unison.

We arrived at Larry's house in the late afternoon and were shown to our room. When we walked out onto the patio, Larry was sitting by the pool with a woman and another couple. They were dressed up for dinner, Larry in casual-chic attire—Ralph Lauren and Gucci—the others in a gaudy Californian style that flaunted their money. Larry was in his early fifties and looked as handsome as ever. A bit of gray in the hair and fine lines at the corner of the eyes even enhanced his looks.

He got up to greet us.

"Here you are! Welcome!" He kissed me. "Hi, sweetie. So good to see you."

He shook hands with Jim. "And this is the lucky guy who snatched you from *bella Italia*. Pleased to meet you."

"How d'you do, sir." Jim accompanied his words with the hint of a bow.

Notwithstanding his locker room talk in everyday speech,

Jim was an accomplished gentleman when circumstances called for it. It came natural to him, as a result of his southern upbringing. On those occasions, his impeccable manners gave him a romantic flair, a retro charm one may find in nineteenth-century novels with heroes stirred by passions and conflicts. And even in everyday life, the swearwords he used to blend in with the guys had an odd ring in his mouth.

"You may call me Larry. We're among friends here. This is Jenny Whyte, the literary critic of the *City Scene*, and these are the soon-to-be lucky owners of this great property, Bob and Susan Stone. Bob is a Hollywood producer."

We all exchanged greetings and smiles.

"I guess Miguel has already shown you your room," Larry continued. "He and his wife, Anita, take care of the house in my absence, and of me when I'm here."

"He's been very nice. We've already taken a shower and are ready for dinner. I'm starving." I suddenly realized that we hadn't had any food since early morning.

"Dinner's coming. I asked Miguel to set up a buffet right here by the pool."

The view from the deck was magnificent. The Mission-style mansion stood on a cliff in Hope Ranch, with the back to the ocean. From that vantage point we could see the lights of the Waterfront on the left, and the fiery colors of the sunset on the right. A picture perfect view, like in the postcards the tourists bought in the souvenir shops on Cabrillo Boulevard.

The margaritas were mixed and chilled to perfection.

"Do Miguel and Anita come with the house?" Susan asked. "I'd be willing to raise our offer if they do. These margaritas are superb."

"I take credit for it. I mixed them myself," Larry said. "As for Miguel and Anita, you're out of luck. They have other plans."

"Other than being sold?" Jim asked. He could not help being provocative if faced with vulgarity, even when he was in polite mode. I cringed and braced myself for the worst.

Everybody laughed hesitantly to disguise their embarrassment, except for Bob who burst out laughing.

"Ha ha ha... This is a great line for a script. Have you considered becoming a screenwriter?"

"I'm a scholar, and I write academic books."

"What difference does it make? We need new talents in Hollywood. Come see me one of these days... Ha ha ha, what a great line!"

"Tell me about your latest book," Jenny asked. "I may consider reviewing it for the *City Scene,* although our readers prefer light fiction."

"Thanks. But I don't think it's suitable for your readers. Besides, it's not been published yet."

I sent Jim an incinerating look that he deflected and ignored. He had already managed to insult the two ladies and he seemed intentioned to continue on that course.

"Oh good, dinner's ready," Larry intervened, having caught a signal from Miguel. "Please go and help yourselves."

This announcement came at the right time to relieve the tension.

Everybody's attention turned to food. The display had the colorful look of a Mexican painting: avocado and mango salad, abalone shells with lemon wedges, dark red gazpacho. Anita presided over the arrangement. Miguel, at the grill, cooked the halibut steaks, thick and tender.

We sat down at a large table under the colonnaded porch that separated the pool area from the house. Now the sun had disappeared in the ocean and a blanket of stars covered the sky.

"It's so beautiful here." It sounded like a platitude, but I was expressing my genuine feelings. I touched Larry's hand. "Are you sure you want to sell?"

Susan jumped in. "Don't give him any ideas. God forbid he'll change his mind. We've been working very hard for months through our agent, trying to convince him."

Larry looked unhappy. "It was a difficult decision," he said.

"Well, in the end we made him a very generous offer. There's nothing money can't buy," Bob said lighting up a cigar.

"I disagree," Jim retorted. "There is something that can't be bought. Beauty, for example. You can buy a beautiful object, even an exquisite work of art. But you may not be able to own its beauty if all you can see is its price."

Bob was puzzled. "What d'you mean?"

I came to the rescue. "Bob, would you be so kind as to pour me some wine?"

He welcomed the interruption and turned to me. "D'you like California wines?"

"They're okay. Many come from Italian grapes that have been transplanted here, but the final product is not exactly the same. It cannot be. It depends on so many factors. I can tell you more about it if you're interested…" and I proceeded with a long story about Villa Flora, where Amy and I spent so many summers, the vineyards, the winery, the air and the soil. The story was meant to keep him busy and shielded from Jim's attacks. Larry joined me with his memories of those faraway days when he used to come and visit, and taste the new wines.

There was excitement in the whole household every time a phone call announced Larry's arrival. Amy would go and round up the kids from the neighboring villas to show them what an extraordinary dad she had… so special… so American… And he never disappointed her. She used to say, "I wish I were mom, then I'd marry him and we'd stay together all the time." She did not understand why Anna preferred to live by herself. And yet, when he was there she seemed to enjoy his attentions. She was radiant in the morning. They slept together in the Cupids suite, which was used only on rare occasions. *Signora* Amelia ordered Rosa, her most trusted maid, to prepare it for the couple, although Anna objected, "Mother, no need for that, we can use my room." But at Villa Flora *signora* Amelia ran the show. And so, Rosa thrust open the French doors to the upper terrace to let the sun in, made the bed with the finest linens and filled the porcelain vases with flowers from the garden. The Cupids, frolicking in the thick of the woods over the walls, or balancing on intricate garlands around the cobalt-blue ceiling, took aim at the lovers with amorous arrows. Larry used to say that he would fall under the spell if he were not already in love.

During harvest days, Amy and I took him for long walks in the vineyards. He knew nothing about grapevines and their cultivation, and often stopped and talked to one peasant or another to learn something. But he spoke only a few words of Italian, and those were totally inadequate to communicate with the locals. Those good people interrupted their labor, stood up, wiped the sweat from the brow, and stared at the American with a blank look. Then they asked us, "What he say?" At times, just for fun, Amy would make it up. Like when she told them, "He said he really likes the wine you make and he'll take you all to America so that you'll make the same wine over there." That was received with an outburst of joy among the young and an encouraging nodding among the older ones. It was Larry now who stared at the scene with a blank look.

Jim sat across from me, between the two ladies who seemed not to mind his quips. Actually, they both later said that they found him charming because of his passionate nature and disarming honesty. The two ladies were laughing now; Jim had a keen sense of humor. I could not hear their conversation because I was still involved in the discussion on wine making, but my eyes were on him.

He handled the food with effortless elegance and a sure

sense of etiquette, as always, whether we were in an upper-crust restaurant or at the university cafeteria. He had beautiful hands, strong but finely shaped, which added a sensuous touch to his every gesture. Those were hands that knew how to caress a woman.

"Larry, we need your help," Jenny called out from across the table. "I've arranged for a horseback ride in the Mission Canyon tomorrow, but Susan insists that we all go out on their boat to the Islands. What d'you say?"

"I'll take the boat out, no matter what," Bob answered without being asked.

"Let's see what our young friends want to do," Larry said diplomatically.

I declined for both of us before Jim had a chance to speak. "Both proposals sound wonderful, but we cannot join you. Bob Kennedy is going to speak here tomorrow and we want to go to the rally. Right, Jim?"

"Yes, of course," he hastened to agree. Even a political rally now seemed to him like a preferable alternative.

"In this case, I'll come with you," Larry decided.

Jenny looked disappointed, and soon after dinner she left, declining Larry's offer to see her home.

The next day, twelve o'clock, we were on the lawn of the Sunken Garden at the Courthouse. The garden, which occupied an entire city block, was filled to capacity. Many in the crowd were young people and minorities, but there were folks of all ages, ethnicities and walks of life. We found a place near the steps leading up to the main archway. That's where Kennedy was about to come out from any minute now.

City authorities and local politicians alternated at the microphone, but nobody paid attention to them. The people were waiting for *him*.

Larry was in a good mood, more relaxed than the night

before. Obviously, he enjoyed being alone with the two of us.

"You're not angry with me for having spoiled your date, are you?" I asked.

"On the contrary. You know, Jenny was my sweetheart when we were young, and over the years we renewed the... acquaintance, so to speak, every time I came back home—even if she was married most of the time, and not necessarily to the same husband."

"And you didn't want to 'renew the acquaintance' last night?"

"I thought I did. But I was glad when she left after dinner."

"Here he comes," Jim said.

A group of people came out onto the platform at the top of the steps—political associates, campaign managers, body guards—and behind them the boyish-looking, charismatic leader who set millions of hearts and minds on fire.

The crowd burst out in applause and then began to clap rhythmically to the chant of "RFK," "RFK"...

He stood center stage, now alone, his red-golden hair glistening in the sun. A large smile brightened his face.

"We want Bobby," "We want Bobby"...

He began to speak. He reiterated the main themes of his platform: racial equality—"Let's have a reconciliation between the races..."—economic justice, social programs to alleviate poverty and improve education—"We should work together, no more divisions..."—emphasis on human rights in domestic and foreign policy, aid to poor countries and military disengagement—"We want peace in Vietnam..."

"RFK," "RFK"...

"With your help, we can do it. Thank you to those who worked hard across the state during this campaign, and especially to the young who are the future of the nation. And thank you also to all my friends in the black community. The day after tomorrow, we'll celebrate our victory."

"We want Bobby!" "We want Bobby!"

He waved. He was gone.

The people began to disperse. We slowly moved with the crowd toward the exit. Fragments of conversation floated above our heads: "He's what we need…" "Someone with vision…" "A new start for our country…" "He'll get us out of Vietnam…" "He was a friend of MLK…" "He's a friend of blacks…" "He'll bring the country together…" "His policies will help the poor, bring about social justice…" "He has an infectious smile, reminds me of his brother…"

"What d'you think?" I asked Larry. "I don't have a clear sense of this country, yet. Will he make it?"

"He'll make it here in California, and possibly win the nomination. He's not the party's favorite, but he enjoys enormous popular support. Look at this crowd. He speaks their language. He fires them up with his energy and charisma."

"What really works for the people is that he's not a phony," Jim said. "He really believes in the ideals that inspire his speeches. His words ring true, and this has an irresistible appeal. Larry's right that he may win the primary. But then, the general election is another story."

"Why? Don't you think he'll win the general?"

"I think the contest will be tough. Look, America is big and diverse. What appeals to some does not appeal to others. A good half of the voters find his liberal platform too idealistic, impossible to implement, and therefore, risky, even dangerous. They think it would encourage anarchy and cause an economic downturn. And they may in fact be right."

"But those are the conservative ideologues who resist change no matter what."

"Not necessarily. There are many concerned citizens who see Kennedy as the champion of the juvenile movement, the campus disorders, and the Kumbaya gatherings. They'll support the Republican candidate if he's a strong figure who pledges to restore law and order."

"D'you agree?" I asked Larry.

"Jim's right. Most do recognize the fundamental principles of justice, equality, and peace. At the same time, they struggle with the pragmatism of the situation. And the situation may easily get out of hand and turn violent. We'll see the formation of left-wing militant organizations, like in Europe. Not to speak of individual violence. We're still under shock for what happened to President Kennedy, and, only a few months ago, to Dr. King."

"Would you vote for a Republican, then?" I asked.

"Perhaps. It depends on the candidate, but I don't rule it out."

"And you, Jim?"

"No. I'll vote for Kennedy, even knowing that the moment he's elected I'll become his critic number one. For sure, I'll be mad at his policies. But I share his basic principles, and for me it's a matter of making the moral choice, rather than the political choice... That's how stupid I am."

Two days later, back in LA, we spent the evening at the movies. Jim's students had arranged to go see *Bonnie and Clyde* and asked us to join them. Afterwards, the group discussed the film over coffee and pie at Sambo's.

"This is powerful stuff, man. I've never seen anything like that at the movies before."

"I sort of like them. I know they were outlaws, but still... so attractive. I really empathized with them."

"I did too. Look, they robbed banks alright, but their actions were directed against the establishment, an unjust society. There is a parallel with our aspirations today. That's why I like them."

Jim intervened. "But eventually they get killed. How d'you read their death in the end? Just as melodrama, or as something of deeper significance?"

Jim's question opened up a new round of speculations.

"It shows how hateful the establishment is."

"Yes, it's a scene of cop brutality. To kill them like that... like dogs... without a trial..."

Jim: "So, violence is not pretty. Is that what you're saying? But then, why didn't it seem so ugly when they were the ones murdering people?"

"Well, it depends on how it's filmed."

Jim: "Exactly. The death sequence has been shot in a way that reveals the true nature of violence. It's been filmed with four cameras from four different angles, at different speeds, and then edited to expand real time, multiplying the effect of every bullet and magnifying its impact on the flesh. Bonnie and Clyde are not just killed, they are slaughtered. Nobody has filmed violence in this way before. This is brand new cinema, truly revolutionary. And not because it tells the story of two folk heroes rebelling against society, but because it demystifies the romantic notion of 'good' violence."

"I didn't see it that way. Now that you point it out..."

"I was just deeply shocked by that scene. I'll have to think about it."

Jim: "That's what you should do. Think about it."

On the way home, we heard on the radio that Kennedy had won the California primary. We rushed in, hoping to catch at least part of his speech on TV.

Our friends were sitting before the screen in silence. Cindy turned toward us, tears streaming down her face. "Bobby's been shot," she sobbed. The next day he was dead.

After that, the gates of hell burst open. The Democratic Convention in Chicago turned into a battlefield, ensuring Nixon's victory in November. Radical groups became more militant. Confrontations with the police became more violent. The National Guard turned into a deadly force. With the reinstatement of the draft, student riots raged across the nation. Black unrest ravaged the inner cities. The war escalated and later extended to Cambodia.

Stella's Story: Chapter 5
LA, Summer 1970

The cars proceeded at a snail pace along the driveway in that warm summer night. The Worthingtons were having a big party for their fortieth anniversary. They did not want to wait for the canonical fifty years to celebrate their marriage in gold. Rather, they did it regularly every ten years, to remind themselves of how happy they were together.

That's what Marjorie told me. We had become close friends since we met two years ago, notwithstanding the age difference. Perhaps I was looking for a surrogate mother. Often I thought of what Amy told me when we were kids, just before she went to New York the first time. She said that I didn't want to go because I was scared, and that the minute I got there I'd freak out and start crying for mom. I still felt that way as an adult when things got difficult and I could not cope.

Marjorie was the anchor I needed. She provided me with a home away from home. We spent long afternoons on her veranda when I had some free time, curled up on the aqua-colored couches, sipping mango juice and discussing our lives.

"Well, darling," she would start, "give me a big smile. I don't want to see long faces around here. Get that bottle from the table, would you, and put a drop of gin in your juice... That's it! I said a drop... I'll take some too. Now, let's toast another beautiful day."

"Cheers! I feel better already, even before the gin. I love it here."

"And so do I. But, remember, you can be happy anywhere, even in the most godforsaken place, because happiness is a state of mind. You have to find it inside yourself."

"I'm looking for it. I'm sure it's there, somewhere in the folds of my brain. One day I'll find it."

"Good girl. Tell me, how's everything at school?"

"It couldn't be better. I've taken my last class and I'm preparing for the prelims. And my dissertation topic has been accepted."

"Lee told me about that. He said you consulted with him and finally chose a topic involving art theory."

"More precisely, 'Aesthetic Theories of the Early Avant Garde Applied to the Visual Arts and Literature.' Steve Collins has agreed to be my advisor."

"Good choice. He's young and ambitious, and well on his way to a brilliant career... He's barely forty and already a full professor. It can really help you to have him as a mentor. But, beware—he's got a crush on you. I noticed it on various occasions."

"Well, he's not the only one... I know how to handle men's advances."

"I'm sure you do. Besides, it would be difficult for anyone to compete with Jim. He is such a charmer."

Marjorie was right. Objectively, Steve paled when compared to Jim. He was not bad looking, but had an ordinary face, like millions of others. While Jim had a face that was one in a million. Like Brando says in *On the Water Front*, "Some just have faces that stick in your mind."

"Jim's a big flirt, and women like him for his throwaway charm," I said.

"No doubt. But, to be fair to him, his charm is not just the result of a nonchalant attitude. It comes from within. I grew quite fond of him in these two years. He's a good person, fundamentally good."

"Yes, he's honest to a fault. And he often gets in trouble for that."

"His strength is also his vulnerability. It's obvious that the bravado he puts on is a form of self-defense."

"I agree. At times I feel a great tenderness for him, like for a child. But he's moody. He takes me on an emotional rollercoaster. One moment he dazzles me with his intellectual fireworks, he has a brilliant mind, then he can be funny and makes me laugh, he makes me feel at the center of the universe. The next moment he turns against me, for no good reason, just a petty incident. Sometimes he gets in a funk and doesn't get out of it for days. I can't make sense of it. And this bothers me."

"Well, all creative people live in a world of their own that others don't understand. That's the way he is, and you cannot change it. Ultimately, it's up to you to decide whether you want to share your life with him or not. But let me tell you one thing: he loves you, and he's absolutely loyal to you. Those occasional flings you told me about don't mean anything."

"I know that. 'We're a team.'"

"Which is not a bad way to be."

"How was it with you and Lee at the beginning?"

"It was nothing like this. In those days there was a different idea of the couple. Now you may see each other as partners with equal responsibilities, but back then it was not the case. Lee loved me dearly and cared a lot about me. He felt responsible for my happiness and wellbeing, and he assumed the leading role. For my part, I was happy to put him first, to help him succeed, even if I had to renounce my career. I graduated from music school, one of the best in the country, with a degree in piano. My teachers thought I had talent and helped me get engagements with top-notch orchestras. But then, I met Lee. After we got married and had the first child, he expected me to take care of the family. He never asked me in so many words, but I knew it. It was the right thing to do."

"Did you ever regret it?"

"No. What's the point? I've been happy with Lee. And besides, I still have the music. I play for myself, and I taught my sons, although neither one of them became a musician. The one in Boston is a lawyer, and the other is a civil engineer in Ohio... must be boring."

"I never met them."

"You'll have a chance pretty soon. They're coming home for our fortieth anniversary, with their families. The children are teenagers now, some are already in college. We don't see them so often."

Inching my way to the main entrance, I left the car with the valet and entered the large foyer leading to the great hall. An elegant crowd filled the space and spilled over into the music room, the library and the veranda. Marjorie was entertaining a group of guests when she saw me. She came over.

"You look splendid tonight! But why so late? And where's Jim?"

"He apologizes and sends his best wishes. An unexpected occurrence... He couldn't help." The excuse sounded hollow.

"Apologies accepted. But you'll have to tell me the 'true' story later. Come, have a drink."

At the bar a teenage girl asked for a Martini.

"Julia, you're not supposed to drink. Not in my house, anyway," Marjorie scolded the young lady.

"Come on, grandma. I'll be twenty-one in just two years. I'm very close. What's the difference? It'll be just one drink. I promise. Just pretend you didn't see it." She kissed Marjorie on the cheek. "You're the best granny." She left, drink in hand.

Marjorie followed her with a concerned glance. "I don't know how to handle this. And her parents don't know either."

"Just say no," I told her, not knowing the facts.

"It's not so easy. She's recovering from a traumatic experience and is having a difficult time."

"What happened?"

"She's a student at Kent State. A freshman, you know. She was on campus the day of the riot. It was in May, just a month ago. The campus is still closed."

"Now I understand. I've been shocked by those pictures. Was she out there when the Guard came in?"

"Right in the middle of it. She was among those who protested the expansion of the war to Cambodia and the drafting of young men into a war they oppose. When the Guard started shooting she heard the bullets pass her head and saw several students go down. Twelve wounded and four dead, according to the reports."

"It's terrible. What really stuck in my mind is the photo of the girl screaming over the dead body of a fellow student that was widely reported in the media. It says it all."

"That student was shot in the mouth. Julia knew him. He was in the same class with her boyfriend."

"I'm so sorry. And now the protest is spreading all over the country. Have you heard that hundreds of campuses nationwide have joined the 'student strike,' and the National Guard has intervened again, shooting and stabbing the protesters with bayonets? Apparently, in downtown Washington a mob of 100,000 transformed the city in a battlefield, smashing windows, burning cars, slashing tires... The military was called up to protect the White House, and Nixon was taken to Camp David for two days in order to remove him from danger. I don't know how all this is going to end up."

"I'll tell you how it's going to end up. Soon they'll establish a Commission to study the campus unrest and make recommendations on how to quell it. Some scapegoats will pay a symbolic price, the students will get tired of being beaten, and gradually everything will go back to normal. But a 'new normal.' This experience will leave a permanent scar on the nation. As for Julia... we'll be there for her."

Marjorie clicked her glass against mine. "Cheers! Enjoy yourself." She stepped away, but suddenly turned around and said, "By the way, Steve Collins has asked about you." Then, she joined Lee, who stood in the great hall among the university VIPs.

I went out to the veranda, looking for a familiar face to start a conversation. At a party like that it is essential to be seen chatting with someone and having a good time—even if the person's a drag and you're about to collapse because of boredom and high-heel pain.

I leaned on the rail breathing in the balmy air from the garden. It was dark out there, except for a few spots brightened by lights discretely hidden in the bushes—glowing islands on a black lake. What will I tell Marjorie when she asks about Jim? The 'true' story, she said. But I was not sure what the 'true' story was.

"Stella! I'm home," Jim called from the bottom of the stairs, as he walked in. Now we lived in a rented house next to the freeway, pretty shabby but cleared of roommates, kids, and dogs.

"It's only 5 o'clock, dear. It won't start till 7:00."

"You asked me to come home early."

"I still have to blow my hair dry."

Jim was now in our bedroom. "You look beautiful already." He kissed me on the nape of the neck. "Your hair smells good."

"Don't get any ideas, love. I'm busy now."

He moved away and sat on the edge of the bed. "Why did you ask me to come home early?"

"Just to be safe, so that we wouldn't be late."

"Last time we were late it was because you forgot your earrings and we had to come back. Don't put it on me."

"I'm not putting it on you. I wanted to give us plenty of time, that's all. Just relax."

"*I* should relax?! Look at you, all pumped up because we're going to the Worthingtons'..."

"They are nice people."

"This is true. But it's also true that they have status, connections, and provide you with a stage where you can shine."

"So what? It's very Italian to mix life and theater. I love to get out of my jeans, put on designer clothes and stand out in a crowd. What's wrong with that?"

"Nothing. You do it with grand class. It shows your natural elegance. But I couldn't care less..."

"Well, let's not discuss life-styles now. Come on, get dressed. I had your suit pressed."

"I'm not going anywhere."

"What?!"

"I'm not going."

"This is rude. You accepted the invitation and now you're cancelling at the last minute? What am I going to tell them?"

"Tell 'em I'm a fucking maniac who doesn't deserve their kindness. Alright? Go! And leave me alone."

When I was ready, I went out the back door without saying goodbye. Jim was lying on the couch in the living room, immersed in reading.

I don't know if he heard me leave.

"The arch frame, the dark background, your head in the foreground... an exquisite portrait. I can't stop admiring the perfect Renaissance aesthetics of your pose." He was standing a few feet from me, like someone who had been watching for a while.

"Oh, Steve. You startled me..."

"You were immersed in deep thought. I guess you were not thinking about the dissertation."

"Actually, I think about it all the time. I dropped by your office this morning but you were not there."

"Sorry I missed you. Come by tomorrow, and we'll have lunch at the faculty club."

"I will. It's nice of you."

"May I replenish your glass?"

"No, thank you. I'm driving."

"Driving your old car? You had some problem with the cooling system, if I remember it correctly. Is it okay now?"

"Not really. I can't find a reliable mechanic."

"Well, let me help you. My mechanic is a great guy. I'll take you there and make sure he does the job and doesn't charge you an arm and a leg. What d'you say?"

"I don't know… If it doesn't take too much of your time…"

"Not at all. I'll make an appointment for tomorrow after lunch. But tonight, let your husband do the drive. You know, men are better equipped to deal with this sort of problems."

"He couldn't come. And besides, Jim's not my husband. I mean, we're not married."

"I apologize. I made an obvious, but indiscreet assumption."

"It's okay. Everybody does. Actually, I even like it because it helps me to keep men at a distance."

He took a step back. "Am I at the right distance? Should I move further back?"

"Don't make fun of me. You know what I mean. I wouldn't think of you as one of the 'men.' You're my professor."

I caught a funny look on his face, between surprised and hurt.

"See you tomorrow around noon. Have a good time tonight," he said curtly. And ignored me for the rest of the evening.

I got home without any trouble.

Jim was in bed, apparently asleep. When I joined him in the dark, he turned to me and pulled me close.

"I'm sorry," he whispered. "I'm terribly sorry. I always end up hurting you. Forgive me."

We kissed. Everything was in that kiss: his regret, my forgiveness, our love. That night we made love as though we wanted to renew our commitment. And it was passionate, and sweet.

A couple of months later I found out that I was pregnant.

Stella's Story: Chapter 6
LA, Fall 1970

Doug and Carol came over for dinner. Without the children, Jim specified—get a babysitter, or take them to granny, or whatever, but don't bring them over, nothing against them, they're nice kids, but let's have a quiet evening among adults, please.

And yet, he liked the children and they adored him. The previous weekend we had a picnic on the beach, at night. Linda and Ricky fought for the best place, the closest to Jim around the bonfire. They would take the food only from him. Afterward, we walked to the pier, looking for ice-cream. Jim and the kids were a few steps ahead. The kids hung on Jim's hands, one on each side, trotting along and talking loudly to overcome each other's voice. There was a full moon. Its cold light painted the landscape in greyscale.

Jim pointed to it. "Can you see our flag over there?"

"Where?"

"Where?"

"Right there, on the moon."

"No. I can't see it."

"I can't see it."

"Well, it's there. Trust me. One of these days we'll take a trip to the moon and go see it. What d'you say?"

"Yeah!"

"Yeah! When d'we go?" Linda asked.

"It'll be some time. The spaceship is not ready yet. I'll let you know as soon as it is."

"When I grow up I want to be an astronaut, so I can go to the moon every day," Ricky said.

"Me too."

"No, you can't. You're a girl."

"But I'll put on the baggy suit and the helmet, and no one can tell."

"Very likely, when you two grow up, there'll be boy astronauts and girl astronauts. No difference. And you'll go riding together among the stars."

"I'll build a house on the moon, a big, big house, and invite all my friends," Ricky said.

"And I'll plant a garden because there are no trees over there. It looks pretty empty, like the beach, and then I'll go bouncing around like on the trampoline, like those men on TV."

"You kids are lucky. Those men charted the way for you. Theirs was an extraordinary achievement. Don't you ever forget."

It was the four of us, no kids. We were in our backyard, under a scrubby magnolia tree, sipping three-dollar-a-gallon Sonoma-Mendocino wine, and waiting for the lasagna to come out of the oven. Beyond the fence, the access to the freeway ran parallel to the back alley. The cars climbed up the steep ramp in low gear and darted away over our heads. Their rumbling drowned out all other background noises. The day was fading out but it was still hot. A hot October day.

Doug raised his glass. "The occasion calls for a toast. I wanted to bring a better bottle instead of this jug but, you know, money is a problem. Anyway, let's drink to Jim's new tenure-track position at NYU. They have an excellent film school and this is a great opportunity for you, my friend. We're very happy for you both."

"Not so fast," Jim said. "It's good the old man, the chair of the search committee over there, heard of the classes I'm teaching and sought me out, but I haven't signed the contract yet, and I have certain conditions. So, it's not a done deal."

"Watch out, man. Don't miss this opportunity because of some silly issues. Here you have this situation with Crafton, where he keeps you on the faculty because you bring hundreds of students to the department. But he'll forever bar you from getting tenure, you know that."

"He's a jerk."

"And you depend on him."

"No, I don't. I can quit any minute and leave him deep in the shit up to his eyeballs. Because without me, the film program he takes credit for will fall apart miserably."

"You're an asshole."

"And you're a suck-up."

Carol took me by the hand, "Let's go see how the lasagna's doing."

We left. It was nice and cool indoors.

"Thank God for air conditioning," Carol said. "Let those two have a showdown while we take a break."

I took a pitcher of ice tea from the refrigerator and we sat down at the kitchen table.

"How d'you feel?" Carol asked. "We didn't have a chance to really talk after the abortion. Everything okay?"

"Everything's fine. I feel great. I'm more and more convinced that it was the right thing for me. No regrets. I want to thank you again for your support all the way through."

In those days, abortion was still illegal in the U.S. I had turned to Carol for advice because I knew she managed to get one the year before. She and Doug could not afford a third child, and they came to that decision together. By word of mouth, she learned of an organization that would take care of the whole package for a fee. A steep fee. The package consisted of flying to Mexico City and being taken to a spa in a resort town, where abortions were performed in secret. Her experience was successful, and I followed in her steps.

However, it took me a while to make a decision. As usual,

I consulted with Amy. And, as usual, she made me face the situation and take action: "Your career will be affected, and your entire life for that matter. You still have to defend your dissertation, get a job, get established... You're not in the condition to raise a child. And Jim, well, we know his position on kids. He'll accept the child because he loves you, but he won't regard it as a bundle of joy." Only after a lot of swaying back and forth between the romantic idea of motherhood and the practical consequences, I decided to go ahead and get an abortion.

Jim was very supportive all along. He said that the decision was mine and mine alone, and that he would have accepted it one way or the other. He was affectionate and considerate the whole time, and we never had a fight for that whole period. A new harmony reigned between us. He also insisted on covering the expenses.

When I left LA, late in August, I knew what to expect. Carol had given me a detailed account:

"I arrived in Mexico City with an early afternoon flight. Doug couldn't come, it would've been too expensive. And besides, that was a requirement. I had to be alone, no companions. I felt a bit lost because all I had was a phone number on a piece of paper. I was supposed to call from the airport and say, 'I'm one of the tourists for the trip to Cuernavaca.' So, I did. At the other end, a man's voice with a heavy Spanish accent told me to take a taxi, and gave me the address of a hotel. He said to wait in my room till I received a call with further instructions. Click, he was gone. I felt like in the middle of a thriller, you know, the ones that involve drugs or other illicit deals. And, in fact, this was an illegal ring I was caught in. But I was determined and I marched right on.

"The hotel was on the outskirts of town, nothing fancy but new and clean, with the impersonal look of a transit place.

They had a reservation for 'the group' and gave me a room. I sat by the phone, hoping the wait wouldn't be long. Soon I realized I was hungry. I did not have anything to eat after that light snack on the plane in the morning. So, I went down to look for food. Nothing in the hotel, no restaurant, no cafeteria, not even a vending machine. I went out in the street. I saw a desolate landscape. A mall was being built where it was once a lower-class neighborhood of small houses and *bodegas*. The cheerful multicolored constructions were now disappearing under the concrete.

"I turned around and walked back to my room. From the corridor I heard the telephone ring. I rushed in and managed to pick up. The same voice told me to be ready for departure in half an hour, to wait down in the lobby with the rest of the group. Click, gone again.

"I had no idea who the rest of the group was, but when I stepped out of the elevator it became obvious. The huge lobby was empty, except for a few young women in the sitting area, who looked exactly like me. You know, that unassuming but self-confident 'American' look, casual, even banal on the outside, but solid as a rock on the inside. I counted five of them. As I approached, their eyes were on me. 'Is this *the group*?' I asked. They laughed, as if we were sharing an insider joke. 'You're in the right place,' 'What's your name,' 'Care for a Coke? I have a full pack.' Sisters! I felt at home, no longer a lone stranger.

"The van arrived at about five o'clock. The voice now had a body, a stocky man with thick black hair flattened with brilliantine, mustache, and dark eyeglasses. He told us to call him *señor* Antonio. On the way out, he exchanged a glance with the reception clerk to signal that the bill had been paid.

"The ride was short, just thirty minutes south of town. *Señor* Antonio sat next to the driver. He told us, 'I'm taking you to Cuernavaca, a beautiful tourist resort.' Then, he did not say a word for the rest of the ride. He picked up a disc from a box marked 'U.S. Tourists' and put it in the player. The Beach Boys filled the space, *Round round get around/I get around/From town to town...* We occupied the two back rows, chatted non-stop, shared sodas and snacks, and admired the scenery. The road went up winding into mountains covered in forests of pine and holm oak. *Get around round round I get around...* Joanne, who was a professor of Pre-Columbian history, told us that Cuernavaca meant 'city of eternal spring' and that it had been a getaway since Aztec times. Maureen, who was working for a travel agency, said that over the years the town attracted famous Hollywood actors, also rich Mafia bosses, and many of them became residents. More recently, she said, the town became the center of the psychedelic movement because of a special mushroom that was growing there, and many artists, writers, or just hippies moved in. But mostly, she said, the town was the favorite country retreat of well-to-do Mexico City residents.

We did not see much of the town because when we got there it was dark. And also because the van skirted it, and stopped at an isolated hotel far out in a thick grove. The build-ing was a two-story construction in hacienda style, with a large patio in the front. A woman came out to meet us, and *señor* Antonio delivered us to her as if he were the carrier of a shipment. After that, he turned around and the van left. The woman was middle-age and attractive, with the slick look of an international tour operator. Her English was excellent. She escorted us inside and into an office. She asked us if we had the money. That's what she said, 'You got the money?' Each of us put on the table an envelope with an amount in cash that we had prepared in advance. She verified the envelopes and put them in a safe. Then, she gave us our marching orders. We'll be shown to our rooms–three to a room. No dinner. Time for a shower and we'll be taken to the 'treatment' room. After the treatment, we'll be wheeled back to our rooms, where we'll be sleeping through the night.

At that point I was a bit scared but I didn't have the time to linger on that. Everything happened so quickly. Thinking about it in retrospect, I realize things could have gone very badly. There were no tests. Everything was done in a hurry, without the backup of proper hospital equipment. I don't know who those doctors were, perhaps they were not even doctors. I was heavily sedated and unconscious throughout the whole procedure, but before going to sleep I saw two figures in white getting busy around my bed. I don't have any other memories. I woke up in the morning feeling surprisingly fine and rested. Maureen and Joanne, who were my roommates, were already chatting and comparing notes. It turned out that the treatment had been the same for all of us. We were taken to the 'treatment' room one after another like on an assembly line. One thing I can say is that those doctors did a good job. Obviously, they had years of practice with hundreds of patients. Nevertheless, we were lucky. Imagine if one of us died. It could happen, she would disappear and never be found again. Even if someone started an investigation in the U.S., it would've been almost impossible to break through the many layers of protection around the organization. Anyway, I don't want to scare you now with these thoughts. We went through a quick checkup and were declared fit and ready to go.

A buffet breakfast with continental food and tropical fruits had been set up on the patio. Waiters in Mexican costumes stood by to assist as needed. Most of us were hungry and kept going back and forth to replenish their plates. I was among them. Others did not recover so well and suffered from a slight nausea. Peggy in particular, she must have been eighteen or nineteen, had no interest in the food. She looked depressed and didn't talk. We tried to cheer her up, but it was clear that she was having second thoughts about the baby. I felt sorry for her. For a woman that young it could be a traumatic experience.

After breakfast we were packed in a van, a different one. No more *señor* Antonio, just a driver who gave us a quick tour of the town to keep up with the excursion charade—the Palacio de Cortes, the Morelos Gardens, the Cathedral, the local handicraft market—and took us back to Mexico City airport."

I went through precisely the same routine as Carol, pretty risky and pretty expensive. But just three years later, *Roe v. Wade* made it possible for American women to get an abortion legally and safely, without having to embark on a shady Mexican adventure. At the same time, it opened up a controversy that divided the nation into two camps, and is still festering to this day.

The timer went off. Time to take the lasagna out of the oven. Carol started fussing around, getting everything ready on a large tray.

From the window, I saw that Jim and Doug were engaged in a game of frisbee. Poor Doug, he was no match for Jim—slightly overweight, in a loose shirt and baggy shorts, he jumped around in a clumsy way like a big puppy.

Jim was bare-chested and barefooted, wearing just a pair of tight jeans. His movements were supple and under control, as if he were rehearsing for a modern dance performance. Every jump, bend, run, sprint, spin, stop… perfectly coordinated. Every move sliding smoothly into the next one. His muscles extended and contracted under the tight skin like musical instruments following the rhythm of a score. His was not just a great athletic body. It was a body that possessed the grace and the overpowering strength of a wild cat, together with its fatal appeal. It was the body of a young lion.

And then, there was the other side of him. I knew what kind of conditions Jim had in mind when he referred to his job offer. He told the committee that his wife was a doctoral candidate and already had a job lined up, and that he could consider moving over there only if she were offered a position as well. I found out after the fact, and I was moved but did not know how to express it, and so I asked, "Why did you do it?" He shrugged. "We're a team." Then, he cradled me in his arms.

"Come on, let's go. Give me a hand." Carol was already on the doorstep with her heavy load. "Get the bread basket and the other small stuff. The guys must be hungry."

A lamppost cast a bluish light on the lawn and attracted swarms of moths. Flashes of headlights from the freeway glided over the edges of the yard.

"Coming," I said. And we joined the guys in the heat of the night.

The deal with NYU did not go through because Jim decided to reject the offer when it was clear that there was no position for me. It was winter now, rather cold even in LA. We were at home, like most evenings, working on our respective projects.

A knock on the door resonated loud in the silence. TV, radio, and players were off. The only background noise was the rumbling of the cars on the freeway and the ticking of our typewriters. It was around 8 p.m.

"I'll get it," Jim said.

He picked up a baseball bat and went to the door. You never knew who might be out there in those days. The members of the 'Manson family' implicated in the murder on Cielo Drive had all been arrested, but the horror of that senseless slaughter was still fresh on our minds. 'Helter Skelter' from a benevolent Beatles song had become a sinister spell of doom.

It was Jack. We had not seen him since we moved out of Venice.

"Hi, man. What're you doing here? What's up?"

"I need help, man. Let me in."

I came out to see what was going on. Jack looked even thinner than I remembered him. His hair and beard were overgrown. They looked pitch black against the pallor of his face. His dark eyes shone feverishly.

"Are you okay? Come in, I'll make coffee."

Now we were sipping coffee in the living room.

Jim lit up a cigarette. "Help yourself, man."

"No thanks. I'm gonna roll one up." Jack lay down on the couch. "Can I stay for the night? I've no place to go."

"No problem. You can stay," Jim said, and then glanced at me realizing that he spoke too soon without asking for my consent.

I nodded. "Of course you can stay. You're no longer living in Venice?"

"I moved out some time ago. Went to San Francisco. We've been active there. Small actions, you know, nothing serious, but enough to get in trouble with the police. Those bastards arrested two of our comrades. So, we moved back to LA for the next action. A much bigger one."

"Are you connected with today's bombing of the police station downtown?" Jim asked. It had been in the news all day. A big explosion with no victims, fortunately. The coverage was extensive.

"You can say that, man. I actually built that bomb. Once you learn how, it's easy enough, a piece of cake... although our comrades in the New York last spring blew themselves up in the process, there in the Village. They were the first to die for the cause."

"So, you're with the Weathermen?"

"*You don't need a weatherman to know which way the wind blows...* it came from Dylan's song, you know. Now we call ourselves the Weather Underground. We went underground in order to operate more efficiently. We plan the next move in hiding and then strike with violence and precision."

"But why? What is it that you want to accomplish?"

Jack sat up and hunched over, his back to the lamp. His face was in the dark, but Jim could feel his piercing stare.

"We want to destroy U.S. imperialism and achieve a classless world. The oppressed people, they are the ones who create the wealth of the empire. Therefore, the goal of the revolutionary struggle is the control and use of that wealth in the interest of the oppressed of the world."

"You're reciting a page from Lenin's theory of imperialism. If you want a new world, you need to come up with new ideas. You're just rehashing an old doctrine which has not liberated anyone. It has only replaced an oppressive power with another."

"This really shows your white middle-class mental setup. You obviously don't understand. Blacks are with us because they know what it means to be among the oppressed. But you and your kind need to be sensitized to the cause. That's why we're engaged in this sort of actions. Those bombs should work as a wake-up call. We will create a mass revolutionary movement. Sooner or later everybody will mobilize and join the ranks. Even you, man."

"Kiss my ass! I'll join the Foreign Legion before joining your ranks. You're not going to lay any of that white-guilt crap on me. You said I don't understand. You're damn right I don't. Please explain to me how a bright and educated guy like you can succumb to this self-destructive delusion."

"For me it's natural. I grew up a spoiled brat, the last kid of a filthy rich family, pampered by parents, older siblings, and a team of house servants. When I was a teenager, I began to feel embarrassed by my privileged status. For years, our valet, a black man with white hair, had polished my shoes and brought them to my room every morning. He had even helped me put them on when I was younger. At that time I didn't think anything of it. But, years later, the image of that man kneeling down at my feet kept coming back and sort of bothered me. I felt uneasy. Those were the days of the Civil Rights marches, and there was a lot of talking about that sort of stuff. Then, more recently, I met someone who introduced me to the struggle, and I embraced it."

"But your struggle is very different from the Civil Rights struggle. That was a pacifist movement with a profound Christian component. Yours is a violent movement based on Marxist philosophy. Dr. King had a clear and pragmatic objective, a piece of legislation. You have an abstract objective residing in the realm of utopia. His words had weight, they carried real meaning. Your words are empty slogans..."

"Look, all we want is justice. We want to level the playing field for all mankind."

"By focusing on mankind you won't help that valet of yours. By planting bombs you won't create a peaceful world. To help someone move upwards and have a better life, you must create opportunities for the individual to work and prosper freely."

"We will not allow this country to enjoy peace and prosperity while waging a fucking imperialistic war in Vietnam. We'll bring the war home, and turn it into a civil war that will topple this fascist regime."

I got up and opened the window to let the smoke out. The ashtray was full, and several butts had spilled on the table.

The piercing sound of police cars dashing by over our heads cut the air like a sharp blade.

"The pigs're on the hunt. Soon they'll be here," Jack said, nervously.

"Calm down. They don't know you're here. In any case, you'll be safe in the basement. There's a room in the back that is difficult to find."

I was upset about Jim's offer of protection. "No, it's not a good enough hideout. You'd better get out of town as soon as possible. It may be easier for you to leave now in the dark, rather than later in daylight."

A police car emerged from the underpass, headlights reaching out into our living room like searching beams.

Jack jumped to his feet.

"Shit! They're here." He pulled a handgun from the vest pocket. "I must go. This may become a trap. I must go."

He rushed out the back door, jumped over the fence and cut across the neighbor's lawn. A dog ran after him barking rabidly.

The police car stopped at a house one block down the

street. A woman came out screaming. There was some turmoil. A man got arrested and pushed into the car. It was not
the first time. That couple had a history of domestic violence.

The dog kept barking, now from further away. The animal must have caught up with Jack because we heard him
curse, "Ouch! Let go, you motherfucker." Then, a gunshot.
The barking stopped.

"Help! He shot my dog. Help! A thief...!"

"What's going on?" said one policeman. He started running in the direction of the commotion.

Another police car arrived and stopped in the back alley
by the freeway. Two cops got out and joined the first one running after Jack.

It was not clear what happened next. Soon we heard the
sound of a big crash and saw the glare of a raging fire.

The next day we learned from the news that a man on the
Santa Monica freeway, apparently running away from the
police, had been run over by a heavy-duty truck. The truck
driver tried to avoid him by steering sharply into the fast lane
and collided with a car. The Medical Examiner was unable to
identify the body because it had been reduced to mincemeat
and subsequently burned to ashes in the fire that developed
in the collision. According to a local resident, the news reported, the man had trespassed into his property, probably to
burglarize the house, and killed the dog.

Another piece of news reported that the previous day's
downtown bombing had been claimed by the Weather Underground, and that all members involved in the action remained at large.

Stella's Story: Chapter 8
LA, Fall 1973

I had successfully defended my dissertation that morning. Steve shook my hand in front of the commission and bestowed the academic kiss on my forehead. Then, he escorted me out of the room.

"You were superb. What a performance. They ran out of questions. And, besides, their questions sounded so banal in comparison to the answers you provided. As it turned out, *you* challenged them, not vice versa as it was supposed to be."

"I did well, I know. But you should take some credit for it. You have guided me all along."

"That was my job. And I enjoyed every step of the process. Well, let's see, it's almost noon. Let's go to a nice place for lunch and celebrate the event."

He opened the double glass door for me. Jim was waiting outside, under a large sycamore tree. It was late November, and the foliage was alight in a magnificent symphony of red and yellow tones.

"Sorry, Steve. I can't. Jim and I have other plans for the celebration."

Jim picked up his knapsack and moved over to us.

"Did she pass?" He flashed a sly grin.

"She's been brilliant. I had great expectations, but she exceeded them."

"Well then, 'doctor', you deserve some fun now." He took me by the hand. "Goodbye, Steve, thank you for your support."

As we were leaving, I caught a glimpse of Steve. He lingered on the spot, a hurt look on his face, like a kid who had his lollypop snatched away from him.

The next day we hit I-5 North, headed for Mammoth, the best ski resort in the Eastern Sierra Nevada. It was still pitch dark.

"What time is it?" Jim asked.

"Exactly 3:00 a.m. We're on schedule. We should be on the slopes by 9:00."

"We've got a great forecast for the next two days—fresh powdery snow and plenty of sunshine. Up there someone loves you if he ordered such a perfect weather for this occasion."

"All I know is that someone down here loves me. This was your idea. And you made all the arrangements. You even booked one of the top lodges for the night. It must cost you a fortune."

"Well, don't forget that I too love skiing."

In fact, this was a passion Jim and I shared. I grew up at the foot of the Alps, and I was on skis since early childhood; and Jim was initiated to the sport by his father, who every winter took the three boys to the Rockies and subjected them to rigorous training. "It was not fun in those days," Jim told me, "just sheer torture. Father did it because he thought it was an excellent way to discipline the mind and the body." However, it served him well, because now he was able to handle the steepest drops as a champ.

This was not the first time we went to Mammoth. Actually, we tried to sneak in a trip at any possible occasion. But so far, our excursions had been on the cheap, with ski clubs, student groups, discounted ski lift packages and hostel stays. This time, we were going first class.

In a couple of hours we entered the Mojave Desert.

The Mamas and The Papas had softly put us in a dreamy mood.

All the leaves are brown and the sky is grey
I've been for a walk on a winter's day
I'd be safe and warm if I was in L.A.
California dreaming on such a winter's day.

"Pour me a cup of coffee, would you please?"

"Here, careful, it's hot." I tried to make out the shapes of the sand dunes along the road. "Pity it's still so dark. I can't see anything."

"There's nothing to see at this time of the year. It's not like when we saw it the first time, in full bloom after the spring rains."

"That was a spectacular sight. The cactus flowers seemed to light up the entire desert like thousands of burning cups. You said they looked like vaginas, pulsating with life."

"Did I say that? Not bad as a metaphor. Anyway, now there's no life, only sand."

"But some sand formations are fantastic. In the right light they look like a Surrealist art work. Oh, by the way, this is the area where Antonioni shot *Zabriskie Point*. Can we stop by?"

"It's not so close. It would take us about two hours to get there and back on the highway. Frankly, I prefer to get two extra hours of skiing rather than go visit the set of a film that I consider a piece of shit."

"About the film I don't disagree. It's obvious that Antonioni gave in to pressure from the American producers. It's a commercial stunt."

"Exactly, it's tailor-made to attract young audiences. The kids are supposed to fall in love with themselves on the screen, to identify with those beautiful creatures, an endangered species victimized by a materialistic society. They're supposed to feel sorry for themselves and shed some tears. It's shallow and narcissistic."

"I guess you're not going to pick it for your class."

"I may, just as an example of bad movie making. Actually,

it would be interesting to compare it to his previous film, *Blow Up*, also made abroad with some sensationalism. But that one was a masterpiece. It probed deeply into the question of reality vs. representation of reality, by showing the disintegration of the image through the photographic process. Brilliant."

There were no cars on the road. No life around us. The bright cone of the headlights opened up the straight path ahead as we made our way deep into the valley. Through the window, the sky looked like a vault of black onyx studded with millions of diamonds. They were crisp and cold. And far away. We were alone.

We had left behind the last town on the road about an hour ago, the last point where one could get basic supplies before entering the wilderness. We were half the way to our destination.

"Holy shit, what's that?" Jim slowed down. A man stood in the middle of the road, signaling us to stop. A car was parked on the opposite shoulder.

"Need some help?" Jim asked, getting out of the car.

"Thank you, man. Appreciate your kindness. We've been visiting with friends up north, and got stranded here all night, my wife and I. She's pregnant, you know, she's in labor. It's been cold out here, the temperature went down in the twenties."

The man had long hair, a heavy beard, and a lose cotton shirt in the style of an Indian guru. Jim was getting tense not knowing what to do.

"What can I do for you?"

"We live not far from here, man. It's a commune, called Shining Light. If you can just take us there, then we'll be alright. The brothers'll arrange to come and get the car."

Jim looked at the old Buick that sat on the shoulder like an agonizing pachyderm.

"What's wrong with the car?"

"Nothing. It just ran out of gas. Like human beings, you

know, we too run out of energy and need to recharge. That's what we do at Shining Light. We meditate, we concentrate, and the light comes upon us."

"Look, I want to help but... Shit, to take you home we have to go back all the way to Ridgecrest, and from there go find that godforsaken place in the middle of nowhere... I'm sorry for your wife... I'll stop at the next gas station and call an ambulance."

The woman came out of the car. She was visibly in pain. She stumbled on the pebbles. The man grabbed her and she leaned against him.

"Hi," she said in a soft voice, "thank you for helping us. You're beautiful people."

At that point, I recognized her.

"Cindy! Is it you? I can't believe it..."

We hugged and kissed and howled in disbelief.

It had been three years since she and Ken moved out to the commune, and we had lost track of them.

"What a way to meet again. And where's Ken?"

"He too lives in the commune, but now I'm with Carl. He's our enlightened leader." She took the man's hand and leaned more heavily against him. Then, she suddenly grabbed her belly and suppressed a scream.

Jim made room in the back seat, moving all our gear to the trunk. He had made a decision. He had decided to do the right thing.

"Get in the car. I'll take you to the hospital. The closest one is in Bakersfield. We'll be there in two-three hours."

He made a U-turn and pointed back in the direction we came from.

Cindy was getting progressively worse. She had a fever and could hardly breathe as a result of having spent the night in icy weather.

Carl held her head on his lap and comforted her.

"Don't worry, sister, we'll soon be home and you'll feel

better immediately. The holy atmosphere'll cure you, and our people'll be there to receive the baby as a precious gift."

She just moaned.

Carl tapped Jim on the shoulder. "Hey, man. The lady here's in pain and wants home. So, forget about the hospital. We don't believe in that kind of crap anyway. Just take us home."

"You must be kidding. You jerk. Are you aware that she may die? She may have pneumonia. The hospital's where we go. And if you don't wanna come with us, I'll kick your ass out the car, and you can go crawling home with the rattlesnakes."

There was no reply. For a while, from the back seat, we only heard the sound of Cindy's heavy breathing.

A faint light dawned in the east and rapidly expanded to erase the darkness of the night. Now there was traffic in both directions. Jim proceeded undaunted, focused like a laser beam on his objective.

I put a hand on his thigh. "Are you okay?"

"Fine. Don't worry about me. See if Cindy needs anything."

We got to the hospital around 9:00 a.m. Cindy was taken to the emergency room to stabilize her lungs, and we were told that the labor would still go on for a few hours.

"Hey, Carl. You got a dime to call your holy place? Someone should come and fetch you when we're gone."

"We don't have phones over there. No technology, you know. Machines poison the air."

"Unbelievable! So, what d'you intend to do when the baby comes?"

"I don't know. Someone'll take us home."

"Oh, no. No, no. Not me. We're out of here."

I had been silent until then.

Jim turned to me and asked, "What d'you want to do?"

"Frankly, I'm worried about Cindy. Jim, I know this is a

lot to ask of you, but can we stay a little longer? She'll need a friend by her side when she gives birth."

"Well, what can I say? The day's lost anyway. If we leave in the early afternoon, we'll still be able to enjoy the evening at the lodge and ski all day tomorrow." He wrapped his arms around me. "I'll make you a deal. We'll wait until 2:00. If the baby's not come by then, we'll leave anyway. What d'you say?"

"It's a deal," I said, and gave him a peck.

Jim went to look for a cafeteria. I was taken to Cindy's room. Carl was already there but he was of little help, he had fallen asleep on a chair.

I sat by the bed and tried to cheer her up with small talk and chitchat about old friends—Carol, Doug, the kids, and what about Kevin, he apparently had a one-man show recently, quite successful, and was Hamlet still growing taller…

She relaxed and got into a good mood. Perhaps, this did it. The fact is that around noon a nurse told us that the baby was on its way and wheeled Cindy out to the delivery room. When they brought her back with the baby in her arms, she was radiant.

"A boy or a girl?" I asked.

"A boy."

"D'you have a name for him?"

Cindy looked at Carl and smiled. Then she turned to me.

"Siddhartha," she said plainly, as if the choice was made in heaven.

At 2:00 p.m. we hit the road again. Jim kept going on coffee and cigarettes.

"Are you sure you don't want to take a short nap? I can drive for a while."

"No. I won't be able to sleep. The adrenaline's running high. Just make sure we won't run out of coffee."

I kept talking to keep us awake. "I still cannot believe what happened… To meet Cindy in the middle of the desert, and in those conditions… If it weren't for you, she may not have survived."

"You may be right. But I didn't do it because it was Cindy. I would have done it for anyone. When I saw how sick she was, I had no choice."

"I know that."

"Well, let's not talk about it anymore. Ready for our super-weekend, love?"

"Ready."

When we passed the spot where we met Cindy and Carl, we noticed that the old Buick had been removed, probably towed by the highway patrol.

"Another three hours and we'll be there," Jim said.

As we moved toward our destination, I was taken with the spectacular view of the Eastern Sierra. The valley gradually gave way to the mountain range.

"Look, there's Mount Whitney. We're not far, now." Jim pointed to the massive peak, its snow cap shining under the oblique rays of the setting sun.

It was getting dark. We passed the surreal landscape of the Bristlecone Pine Forest dotted with the twisted shapes of ancient trees, a primitive world that defied the ages. We were immersed in another time dimension. Until, all of a sudden, Mammoth Mountain loomed in the distance in its majestic splendor.

We arrived at the lodge at 7:00 p.m. The posh Grand Lodge scintillated with hundreds of lights against the dark mountain slope. A cheerful stream of people in leisure suits went in and out the revolving door.

We parked the car in the driveway, exhausted but excited at the thought that we finally made it. We could now take a shower, unwind, and open that bottle of French champagne in the ice bucket that looked so alluring in the picture of the suite we saw in the promotional brochure.

"Good evening, sir," the reception clerk greeted us. "Welcome to the Grand Lodge. May I have your name, please?"

"My name is Welsh. James Welsh."

"Oh, I see, Mr. and Mrs. Welsh. Well, sir, it seems that we have a little problem."

"There shouldn't be any problem. We have a reservation. I made it two weeks ago."

"Yes, yes, of course. But check-in time is 3:00 p.m. In order to keep your reservation, you should have called to alert us of the delay. Now... I'm terribly sorry, but according to our reservation policy we had to give your room to another guest. You know, it's a weekend, we have a full house."

"You what?!"

The tension Jim accumulated during that long and eventful day was about to erupt like a volcano.

He kept his voice low and menacing, like in a saloon showdown where the stranger utters the ultimatum, his hand hanging loose over the holster.

"I don't give a damn about your reservation policy. You can take it and shove it, as far as I'm concerned. Gimme that suite. Now."

The clerk was visibly shaken.

"The best I can do, sir, is to give you a room—although not a suite—in our twin lodge, two miles from here. I'm sure you'll like it... And, of course, you can come back here and dine in the restaurant."

"Bullshit! Call the manager."

At that point, I would have given anything for the twin lodge room. I caught a glimpse of the stylish dining room through the glass doors from the lobby, and longed to be seated at one of those tables set with linen and crystal, tended by solicitous waiters, among beautiful people in a festive mood.

The manager came and was apprised of the situation.

"Unfortunately, sir, there's nothing we can do. Our reservation policy..."

The volcano erupted. And the explosion was loud.

"Is that all you can say? Shit! I didn't drive 400 miles through the desert to get here and be lectured on your reservation policy..."

To my embarrassment, several people in the lobby were now watching the scene. They seemed alarmed. Mothers whisked their little ones away.

"Sir, you will get a full refund. And in order to make up for this unfortunate situation, we will not charge for the room in the twin lodge. You and your wife will be our guests."

"We won't stay a minute longer in this goddamn place. We're out of here. Give the twin lodge room to your grandmother, with my compliments."

Jim was already by the revolving door when I caught up with him.

"Jim! Stop! This is foolish, you're acting like a child."

He ignored me. He was out, walking briskly toward the car.

"Jim! Wait!" I could hardly keep up with him.

He was by the car.

"What are you doing? Be reasonable. You can't drive all the way back to LA now."

"Yes, I can."

I grabbed him by the arm and looked him straight in the eye. "Don't do that to me. I will *not* forgive you."

He did not hear me. "You want to stay? Stay! Here, take your skis." He released my skis from the rack and threw them to the ground. "Tomorrow, take the bus, take a plane, hitchhike... I don't care."

He was in the car.

He turned on the engine.

I was barely able to jump in before he darted off the driveway.

"My skis...," I said feebly.

"Fuck the skis. I'll buy you new ones."

* * *

We did not say another word until we got home.

Jim parked the car. He was exhausted and calm. The rage had evaporated.

"What time is it?" he asked.

"It's 3:00 a.m. Exactly twenty-four hours since we left."

He hanged his head and paused for a few seconds.

"I'm sorry," he said. His voice expressed regret for his bout of fury, and also frustration for botching up the special weekend he had so carefully planned as a gift to me.

I did not answer. I felt sorry for him, and at the same time I felt estranged. I got out of the car to hide my tears. That night, I slept on the couch in my study.

"No. That's not good. Please erase, *The viewer may infer the presence of...* The sentence should read, *The insistent repetition of the same chromatic palette creates semiotic color patterns that connote the emotional theme of the painting.*"

I was typing the paper Steve had to deliver at a symposium the next day. He was pacing the room, dictating from a draft he had jotted down on a notepad. After my dissertation defense, Steve had hired me as a research assistant to work on a big project for which he had received a prestigious grant from the NEH. I had applied for a teaching position at several local colleges and, while waiting for an answer, I gladly accepted his offer. I loved the job—the topic was in my area of interest. And there were other advantages. I had a small office, adjacent to his big office, full of light and with a gorgeous view of the Quadrangle's manicured lawn and flower beds.

But occasionally, when the department secretary was not available or when there was an urgent job, Steve asked me to do some typing. "You should say no," Marjorie advised me, when I complained to her. It was not so easy. 'Girls' in my position, even if they had a PhD, were supposed to be nice to male superiors. What's a little typing? And making coffee? No big deal.

I was typing and I was unhappy. Evidently, I could not conceal my feelings entirely because Steve looked at me and stopped.

"What's wrong?"

"Nothing. What d'you mean?"

"You seem to have been under stress lately. It's been a few months now. You look pale, as if you don't sleep well at night. What's going on?"

He was right. It was not just the typing that bothered me. The situation at home was a serious problem. After the trip to Mammoth, something hard to describe got in between Jim and me and pushed us apart. On the surface everything was normal, but an awkward feeling lingered in the air, while un-expressed questions floated over our heads. We tried to find the answers in each other's eyes, but our eyes could not sus-tain the quest. "Are you still with me?" Jim's eyes asked. The doubt in his gaze magnified my own doubt. I averted the eyes, "Do I still love him?" This thought frightened me. I wanted to love him. And yet, when he tried to reach out to me, I retreat-ed. Only at night we would recover the usual intimacy. The passion would take over all questions and doubts, working as a primitive force independent of thoughts and emotions. But in the morning, the uneasiness came back, together with the disconcerting sensation of not knowing what was happening to us, and not wanting to acknowledge that something *was* happening.

"Nothing wrong. Really. I'm just a little tired."

Steve put down the papers.

"Then we should take a break. I don't believe in forced labor. Look, it's almost noon, let's go out and have an early lunch."

"I'm sorry. I told Marjorie we would have lunch together today. We're friends, you know. And we have not seen much of each other lately."

Steve had slowly circled around my desk and was now standing behind me. He put his hands on my shoulders and moved them slowly down, caressing my arms.

"I do care about you," he said.

"What are you doing?" I jumped up and turned to face him.

"Don't tell me you've not noticed the way I feel."

"I have, but I never encouraged you. I made it clear that I love Jim."

"But you are not happy with him."

He touched a raw nerve and a surge of emotion choked me. Tears came to my eyes, notwithstanding my effort to push them back.

He took me in his arms. "I'll make you happy. I'll take care of you. With me you'll be a princess…"

"Stop it!"

He kissed me on the mouth. I managed to turn my face away.

"Stop it, I said!"

I pushed him back and regained my composure. I collected my purse and coat. On the way to the door, I stopped and said, "I'll come back after lunch. I hope we'll be able to work together as if nothing happened. But if for you this is not possible, please be clear and fire me right away."

He was looking out the window at a winter sky dotted with white clouds constantly reshaped by a strong wind. He had his back to me. "Enjoy your lunch," he said curtly.

Marjorie was already there when I arrived at Juanita's Restaurant in Westwood. The décor was Spanish, and so was the food. We ordered *tapas* and two glasses of *vino de mesa*.

"I've got news for you," Marjorie said.

"And I've got news for you."

"You go first."

"No, you go first. My news is not so great."

"Alright, then. Lee has decided to retire at the end of the school year."

"Oh, what a pity! I guess I should say 'congratulations' or

something appropriate. But I can't. What about the students? They're going to lose a great teacher. Why did he decide to retire?"

"He's been teaching for forty years, don't you think it's enough? Besides, he'll be on the Board of Trustees, and therefore still involved in education. But the main reason is that he wants to devote his time to writing the definitive book on the founding of the United States."

"Good for him. It's important to remind people, especially people my age, of the significance of it."

"I agree. But that was not the only news. Listen to this. The Department wants to establish a program in film studies and to open a tenure track position for a young professor who would also serve as the program director."

"Jim has been pushing this project for six years. He practically designed the film program single-handedly."

"This is the point. Before retiring, Lee wants to ensure that Jim gets the position he deserves. He's determined to put all his weight behind him."

"Why? Why would he do that?"

"Because there is no candidate more qualified than Jim. And Lee always recognizes merit and disdains politics."

"Marjorie, this is great! Jim needs all the help he can get. You know that Crafton doesn't particularly like him, although he likes the success Jim's having with his classes because it makes the department look good, and it's a feather on his own hat."

"Crafton is a mediocre person with a huge ego. He needs someone to provide the spotlight for him. Lee will leverage Crafton's ambition and convince him that Jim will further enhance the department's prestige."

"I hope he'll succeed."

"I know he will, trust me."

"Well, I'll be forever grateful to him... to you... I don't even know what to say."

"Don't say anything. Lee is just happy to do what he feels is right and good for the university. But now, I want to hear your news."

"Steve made a pass at me."

"And you?"

"I rejected him, of course. And now, I may lose my job."

"I don't think so. I know him, I had occasion to see him in other situations. At first he takes offense, and then he acts as if nothing happened. But he never gives up. You'll see. He'll keep you on the job and wait for the right time, when your guard is down. And then, he'll strike again."

"I won't let him. I'm sure I can keep him at bay. He's not a bad guy, he's got many good points. It's just that I'm not available, and he must understand that."

"This makes you even more desirable in his eyes."

"What're you saying? That he's interested in the challenge more than he is in me?"

"I'm saying that you should be aware of what's going on, and never forget for a minute that Jim loves you."

When I returned to the office, Steve seemed to be in a good mood. He said that the secretary was going to do the typing and I could go back to my research. He expected to discuss the results the next morning over a cup of coffee, which he offered to make himself.

There was great excitement all over campus. Graduation week. The students strolled around in ceremonial garments, the faculty rushed to convocations in academic regalia. And parents, hordes of parents, trotted behind their children with gleaming faces and puffed up chests.

A special party for Lee's retirement was taking place in the Great Hall, and a buffet had been set up under a tent in the adjacent Lilacs Garden. The hall was crowded with faculty, those who had worked with Lee for many years and those who had known him less closely but nevertheless admired him as a scholar and a person. Also his students came in droves, not the current ones who scorned the establishment, but his former students, now respected professionals and esteemed alumni in their forties.

On the stage, the university president, the provost, and the dean of the school alternated at the podium to deliver their acknowledgment speeches. It was Lee's turn now to make his remarks.

Marjorie was sitting in the first row, together with the senior professors and their wives. Steve Collins was amid them, and so was Craig Crafton. Jim and I sat a few rows behind, next to Doug and the other junior faculty and staff.

In the past six months since the incident, Steve had behaved impeccably: socially courteous, occasionally friendly, always professional. I felt relaxed and comfortable working with him, no longer threatened by unwanted sexual advances. On the other hand, I surprised myself thinking, is that possible that he lost all interest in me? Not that I would feel any different for him, but, let's face it, it's flattering to be an object of desire... And then, I would immediately catch myself and realize how silly those thoughts were.

I never told Jim about the incident, but from the very beginning he had noticed that Steve had a crush on me and used to joke about it. He'd refer to him as 'your hopeless suitor,' 'your serenading beau,' or 'your silent admirer.' He was cool about it. No jealousy. After all, 'we were a team,' were we not? And so, we laughed together at Jim's sarcastic gibes.

Lee concluded his remarks. Applause. Everyone rose and began to move toward the garden.

"He's one of the few that we can really admire. It's sad to see him go," Doug said. "It was great of him to make that big donation to the school to fund the film program. I heard that they'll soon announce the search for a director. Are you going to apply? You're certainly the best qualified. You'll have a good chance."

"I may, we'll see," Jim replied curtly, not wanting to elaborate on the subject.

Since I told him about my conversation with Marjorie, he was having mixed feelings about the whole thing. He appreciated Lee's recognition of his merits, and was glad to have a friend in an otherwise hostile environment. On the other hand, he felt sort of embarrassed, as if to have a friend under those circumstances was the same as to have an unfair advantage.

Doug rushed to the buffet to fill up his plate with delicacies that he had never seen on his table at home. We stayed behind looking for Lee. We wanted to congratulate him before turning to food. He was surrounded by a small crowd of who's-who-in-academia. We hesitated, but Marjorie signaled us to join the circle.

Nobody paid any attention to us. They went on with their conversations, punctuated by sparkling smiles.

The dean raised his glass to toast Lee and Marjorie.

"We lose a professor and acquire a benefactor... actually, two. Lee and Marjorie, I have already officially acknowledged your generous donation to the school. Now, I want to thank you personally. Without your support, this project would not have been possible."

"Cheers!" All the glasses were quickly emptied.

"I, too, want to express my heartfelt thanks," said Crafton. "Because of you two, my vision is now a reality. All my efforts over the years will soon concretize into a solid and prestigious program. I'm extremely grateful to you."

The Dean: "As we are to you, Craig. Let's raise our glasses and recognize Craig Crafton, the project architect. He deserves all the credit for laying the foundation of the film program, and for the highest enrollment we have ever had in this department."

"Cheers!"

"He's stealing your baby," I whispered in Jim's ear.

"Motherfucker..." he muttered.

Marjorie looked uneasy. Her glass was still full. Lee, too, did not join in the toast to Crafton. He grabbed Jim by the elbow and pulled him close. Then raised his glass.

"And we should not forget someone who has actually contributed a great deal to the realization of this project. Jim Welsh has been an essential figure from the very beginning."

Crafton jumped in. "I could not have wished for a better assistant."

"It's nice of you, Craig, to give credit where credit is due," said the dean. He turned to Jim, "Thank you for the support you provided. The new director could certainly use your help when he comes in."

"Let's not jump ahead," Lee said. "There is no new director. We have not even announced the position yet."

"Of course, I was just speaking hypothetically," the dean retorted, surprised by Lee's interference.

The general mood imperceptibly changed from festive to tense. There was an awkward moment of silence.

Jim stepped forward. He stood, feet slightly apart, arms along the sides, clenched fists, a frown shadowing his darting glare.

"Enough of this charade," he stated firmly. He looked Crafton in the eye, "Assistant, you said. Liar! You have a history of stealing other people's work. How many of your publications have actually been written by your 'assistants'? But nobody ever challenged you, because you represent the System in your little, precious department, and to go against the System is the same as to committing suicide. One has to be a bootlicker in order to fit, in order to become a small, well-oiled cog in this monstrous machine. But I do not fit. I've got one thing to tell you, all of you…"—he looked around at the wall of stunned faces—"Fuck you!"

He turned on his heel and was gone.

The group was petrified, dropped jaws and wide-open eyes, like in a freeze frame at the end of a movie. Then, slowly, conversations resumed and people put on a jolly mask to cover the burning insult. Marjorie, though, looked deeply pained, and Lee looked incredulous and hurt. Crafton acted like the innocent victim of a vicious attack.

After the initial shock, my instinct was to run after Jim. But he walked so fast. He had already disappeared beyond the lilacs in bloom. I rushed out of the garden, and stopped. He was nowhere. I got mad at him. "Son of a bitch," I borrowed from his vocabulary. "Why d'you have to put me in this kind of situation all the time?" I felt angry and let down. And yet, I could not help but admiring him for what he did, for his courage to take on the entire department, for his denunciation of institutionalized hypocrisy and cowardice, for his daring stance…

Someone put an arm around my shoulders. My heart bounced… Jim, I thought, and turned to him.

It was Steve. He spoke in a concerned tone.

"Let him go. You deserve better. Come, I'll take you home, my home."

I went along.

Stella's Story: Chapter 11
Fairville, 1974

Steve and I got married in August and moved to Fairville, a small town in the Midwest, where he had been appointed Provost of a large state university.

It all happened very fast. The morning after the scandal in the Lilacs Garden, Jim and I had a confrontation.

"Why didn't you come home last night?" he asked when I walked in.

"Why did you drop me as if I were a stranger? We were there *together*."

"We were together. And now we're no longer. Is that what you want to say?"

"I don't know what I want to say. You're making it so difficult for me."

"Oh, so sorry. You spend the night with your beau, and now you come home and tell me that I make it difficult?"

"I didn't come home. I… I came to talk to you."

"There's nothing to talk about. You must decide which side you're on. Either you're with me, or you're not."

He spoke without anger, with calm determination, but his gaze prompted me, *Yes, yes, say that you are!* He had his hands around a cup of coffee, but I saw his arms stretching out, urging me, *Let yourself go, baby. Come, come to me.*

I made an effort to ignore his call. "Look, I love you, but…"

"But you're leaving me, Stella."

He read my mind and expressed the thought that I could

not bring myself to utter. A curtain of sadness came down on his face. A heavy hand squeezed my heart and made it bleed. I left hurriedly to conceal my tears.

I went back the next day with the excuse of getting some things of mine, but with the hope that, perhaps, it was still possible to get back together, to rekindle the flame and restore the trust, without words, explanations, apologies, just like that, naturally, with a tender embrace.

Jim was gone. He took with him only some clothes and most of his books. He left no note, no forwarding address... Only a silvery eucalyptus twig on my typewriter.

The Provost's residence was a large Tudor house on top of a hill. This was one of the many perks that came with the position. I was expected to be the steward of the property, which was a task that I fortunately loved, and unfortunately poorly understood.

I immediately started to redecorate. I hired a contractor to paint the walls in light colors, take down the heavy drapes to let the light in, and remove the carpeting to reveal the original parquet floors. I also replaced the Victorian furniture with design sofas and chairs, and even ordered from Italian dealers some antique pieces that matched the décor of Villa Flora. The result was... chic.

Steve thought all that was unnecessary, too expensive, and even inappropriate. We were in the heartland and had to blend with the environment, to integrate, not to stand out as foreigners. When I started moving the gilded-framed kitschy landscapes from the walls to replace them with modern art, he got somewhat concerned, although as an art scholar he liked the improvement. But when the portrait of the lady of the house, the wife of the nineteenth-century patron who bequeathed the mansion to the university, was on its way to the attic, he put down his foot and declared that the beautiful dame in the white chiffon dress was an institutional icon, she belonged on the fireplace mantle, and don't I dare touch her.

I relented, and with time I even grew fond of her. Her pensive expression suggested another space beyond the frame. She seemed to follow my movements with a sympathetic eye, and I developed a sort of complicity with the woman who had been in that same role a hundred years before me, and probably shared the same feeling of estrangement in her husband's home.

The decorating work kept me busy during the day. I didn't have a job at the university. Steve asked me to be patient and not push the issue. For the time being, he said, it was much better for his career to have a wife at home, who would project a dignified aura over his domestic life and provide a pleasant environment for official entertainment.

The house decoration also kept my mind off Jim. I did not hear from him since that morning when I hurriedly walked out of our house.

Everything was ready when the time came for the first dinner party. Steve had invited the university president, a dean, and two senior professors with their wives. I had already met all of them on official occasions, and we were supposed to be on a first-name basis: Howard, the president, or was it Harold… and his wife, Jenny, I'm pretty sure; the dean, John, easy enough, with wife Elizabeth; and then… too many names. I asked Steve to help me out, but he frowned, "If you don't remember, just keep quiet and listen."

Howard/Harold looked around in amazement.

"I don't recognize this place. It looks so different. It looks… French."

"She's Italian, honey," said Jenny, looking at me askance.

"Oh, well, you know what I mean." Then, to me, "No offense intended, my dear. I don't find it unpleasant. It's just a different aesthetic."

Jenny jumped in. "I must tell you how much we love Italy. We have been there twice. Once in Rome, for an official visit with the local university. Rome really impressed me, historical monuments on every corner next to *trattorie* with fabulous spaghetti. The second time, we went with a tour—Naples, Pompeii, the Amalfi Coast, all the way down to Sicily. That was an adventure. In the last stretch, before reaching the ferry to the island, something went wrong. We got separated from the group and missed the train where we had reserved seats in first class. We ended up on a regional train that had only the second class, among the local folk. The people there are so picturesque. Across from us there was a middle-age couple. The wife was all dressed in black with a headscarf tied under the chin, just like those characters in the movies. It was lunch time and we had nothing to eat because we were supposed to take our meals in the restaurant car on the other train. So, the husband, a short and stout man, asked us in sign language whether we wanted to partake of their food. When he opened their bag, we realized that they had nothing but oranges. We were embarrassed, but we had to accept in order not to offend them. They were so cute."

"No, not cute. They were poor." I said it curtly, and wanted to add: Those were the same people who half a century ago would end up on Ellis Island. But I checked myself, and wondered why I took her remarks so personally.

Steve steered the conversation in another direction. Over drinks and appetizers, they talked about the year's enrollment, tuition raise, faculty appointments, the new stadium for the football team, co-ed dorms yes or no, and should alcohol be allowed in the faculty lounge.

When we were seated at the table, the conversation switched to politics. Nixon had resigned in disgrace just a couple of months ago, and the country was debating whether the pardon he had recently been granted by his successor was justified.

"I think he should have paid for what he did. It's not a good example for the youth to see our president get off scot-free," said one of the professors.

"I agree with Charles," said his wife.

"That's true. On the other hand, a trial would have tarnished the image of the Republican Party. People tend to identify the individual with the Party," said the other.

"Tom's right," said his wife.

"Look, Nixon may have stretched the law a bit, but those democrats deserved it. They tore the country apart, incited rebellion, riots, destruction. Too bad he made a mistake with those tapes… But he was right about wanting to restore law and order, and for that he had to ensure his own re-election," said the dean.

"John couldn't have said it better," said his wife.

Howard/Harold cleared his throat and weighed in.

"Well, I believe that everybody is equal under the law, and now that Nixon is a private citizen he could have been prosecuted. But the fact that he's been the President of the United States can't be dismissed so easily. A trial would have torn the country apart and generated more division and unrest. President Ford was right when he said that the pardon was in the best interest of the nation, and that it's now time to start the healing process."

"Absolutely correct. That's exactly my view," said Steve.

I kept quiet and thought of the long months Jim and I spent glued to our small, black-and-white TV set, together with eighty-five percent of the American viewers. The three major networks, ABC, NBC, and CBS, covered the hearings of the Senate Watergate Committee live, taking turns every third day, from February '73 to August '74. Friends and students would drop by at any hour of the day with popcorn and a six-pack to join us and camp on the living-room floor.

"Hey man, have you seen *The Washington Post* today? There's another story by those two guys, what's their name, Woodward and Bernstein. Amazing! Where do they get that stuff?"

"Apparently, the source is reliable."

"Who? That 'Deep Throat' mystery man?"

"He's been proven correct so far, which seems to substantiate the rumor that he's from the inner circle, a high-up who wants to stick it to the prez."

"I much prefer the other 'Deep Throat,' that babe Linda Lovelace, you know... Have you seen the movie? I wouldn't mind sticking it down her throat."

"Come on, cut it out, you jerk. We're talking about something serious here."

We were fascinated with what was reported, and how it was reported. Every day a new revelation, the unraveling of the presidency, the arm-wrestling between the president and Congress. Senators from his own party had the honesty of investigating him, and members of his own staff had the courage of speaking out against him.

"Yeah, those guys speak out against him, but they too are implicated in the scandal. Their testimony before the Senate is dictated by the need to protect themselves."

"True. But, at least in John Dean's case, the hearings convey a sense of decency, even regret, recognition of wrongdoing, concern for the abuse of power, and the need to protect the Constitution. Don't you think?"

"I'll give you that. It's now clear to everybody that it's not just the initial crime that matters, but the cover-up that followed."

Jim would point at the Senate hearings, the headlines in *The Washington Post* and other major newspapers, the unrelenting work of the special prosecutor and say with pride and amazement, "And yet, our system works."

* * *

Charles, a professor of political science, was now speaking. "Whatever one may say about the pardon, one thing is certain: our checks-and-balances system and the free media were ultimately able to hold the president accountable for breaking the law. The people won."

"And we should celebrate this victory. However, it may end up being a mixed blessing. It's undeniable that the country suffered a deep trauma that will have serious and lasting consequences," said Tom, a professor of sociology. "For the first time in U.S. history, the unconditional trust that people placed in the government cracked. There were previous crises, of course, discontent and rebellions, but a basic belief had held steadfast for two centuries. The belief that people and government are one, and that those in office, including the president, are representatives of the people and work for the people. Now, we're not so sure anymore."

"But that already started a decade ago, with the cultural revolution sparked by the Vietnam War. That movement began to erode our basic belief, don't you think?," the dean said.

"Perhaps it was a factor, but not a decisive one. That was mainly a youth phenomenon, a counterculture movement that didn't resound with the majority of the population. At most, the majority regarded the war as a mistake, but their faith in the government was not shaken. On the contrary, they considered the protesters as troublemakers, even traitors, as in Jane Fonda's case," Tom said.

I thought Tom had a point. White Americans were still a happy people when I arrived, so different from the Europeans, especially the Italians. In Italy, from time immemorial, the people have regarded the government as a hostile power. The causes are numerous, due to the tortured history of Italy—feudalism, autocracy, foreign occupation—but even in modern times, under a democratic government, the prevalent attitude among the people is one of mistrust and cynicism. The Americans were different. They carried around their happiness like a badge, on their open faces, easy smile, clear eyes, light gait, cheerful greetings... This was attractive and off-putting at the same time. At first sight it seemed to confirm the stereotype existing in Europe of the American as a naïve jolly fellow. But it didn't take me long to realize that their happiness was not a sign of superficiality. On the contrary, those were people of substance, ready to tackle any problem and to meet all challenges head on. Their happiness had a solid basis. It resided in the faith they had in their country and in themselves as part of it.

"When the Americans acquired the knowledge that their president lied to them and betrayed their trust, they lost their innocence," Tom was saying. "It was a fall from Eden. We started seeing ourselves and our government with new eyes. Suspicion and doubt began to erode our faith and, I'm sure, this will lead to a progressive path toward cynicism. In thirty, forty years we will no longer be the same country."

"I am not ready to join in this postmortem," said Howard/Harold. "Our nation is strong, the people are resilient. Did you see how quickly the riots ended after the Paris Peace Accords? No more war, no more riots. The kids were merely against the draft. Now, Ford will follow Nixon's policy of disengagement and in a few months the Vietnam War will be officially terminated, the Watergate scandal will be history, and..."

"And we'll live again in 'the best of all possible worlds,'" Charles concluded.

Howard/Harold looked at him surprised and disappointed, but did not reply.

The dinner was over and the guests left.

"Thank you, honey, for having been such a splendid hostess." Steve put an arm around my shoulders and kissed me on the cheek as we walked upstairs. "If it weren't for that little incident with Jenny at the beginning, it would've been a perfect evening. But you'll get used to it. They're good people and mean no harm. They like you, and they certainly like Italy."

"Then I should've served spaghetti."

"Oh, no, no. The ham roast was delicious and those sweet potatoes on the side were just right. And the cheesecake… to die for."

"Well, we have to thank Dorothy for that." I peered downstairs where Dorothy was clearing the table. "She's local and knows how to please folks from around here. I'd be lost without her help."

We were in the hall by our bedroom door. Steve hugged me and pressed himself against me. I could feel his excitement.

"I love you, anyway. D'you feel how much I want you?" he said, seeking my mouth.

I pushed him back.

"I'm sorry, I have a terrible headache. I'd rather be alone. D'you mind sleeping in the guest room tonight?"

"I do mind. But if this is what you want, I'll abide by your wish. Don't make it a habit, though."

He was mad. I could tell he hardly contained his anger.

"Sleep well," I said, and closed the door behind me.

Stella's Story: Chapter 12
Fairville, 1980

Another hot and humid summer. The damp, sticking to the skin, covered the entire body with a glutinous coat. It was annoying at the beginning, then I got used to it. I even got to like being immersed in that elemental steam bath, fragrant with hundreds of smells—the grass, the flowers, the fruit trees, the grapevine, the softened earth—the smells of my garden. I planted and tended it over the years on the grounds of the Tudor house. I wanted to restore the link to Villa Flora's sensual enchantment.

I succeeded only in part, but Nature herself took care of the rest. I was happy one day when I noticed a lucky clover in the lawn, exactly the same kind we had back home. When I shared these feelings with Amy, she shrugged and said that I shouldn't look back but forward. Our communication line was still open and we kept debating things. With her pragmatic and bold approach she won most of the time. In this case, too, I thought she was right. And kept moving forward—but with my precious baggage of memories in tow.

I lay on the hammock hanging between two huge maple trees, their crowns about to turn into spectacular balls of orange and gold.

Bridget was visiting. She was sitting at the picnic table, filling two glasses of lemonade.

"Come and have a drink, or you'll get dehydrated. Lying for hours in that fishnet like a mermaid caught in the high seas doesn't do you any good."

I joined her at the table.

Bridget was the first local person I met. Soon after my arrival, I was inspecting a suitable spot for my garden, removed from the house, at the far end of the property. The spot included an old wooden shack in disrepair, with holes in the roof and loose planks on the walls. I was struggling with the door, which was overgrown with ivy and wouldn't open.

Bridget's head appeared on the other side of the fence.

"Hi, there! It seems you can use some help, whatever it is that you're trying to do. My husband's very handy."

"Oh, thank you. Would he be willing to give me a hand?"

"He'll do anything I ask him to." She opened a small gate I hadn't noticed and stepped in. "My name is Bridget, and I'm your neighbor."

She was in her sixties, white hair tied up in a bun, round face, round body, round all over, with a warm smile that inspired confidence. She could have been a model for the Good Fairy in a Disney cartoon.

Later, I learned that her family was German and that her grandparents came to the States at the turn of the century, and that she was the first in the family to marry a real American because her husband, Larkin, didn't even know when his ancestors came to these shores. For sure they were already here at the time of the westward migration because there were stories of a great-great-grandfather battling the Indians. They had been farmers for generations, and now Larkin had his own farm and raised horses, and she enjoyed going to the show at the State Fair, and watching Larkin's beautiful Palomino win the first prize. Another thing she enjoyed doing was baking apple pies and German strudel—both equally delicious, as I had occasion to verify a hundred times.

"Thanks for the lemonade. So refreshing. I really needed it."

"Who doesn't on a day like this? Besides, I've known you for six years now, enough to be able to tell what you need and when."

"You definitely know how to take care of me. In this respect, you remind me of Marjorie, my good friend back in LA. She, too, was a surrogate mother for me, but in a different way. Last time I saw her was at my wedding. She came to the reception in a mood that was more appropriate for a funeral. It wasn't much of a reception anyway, just a handful of guests, mostly Steve's friends and relatives."

"And what about your friends and relatives?"

"I didn't have many close friends there, and mother could not come on such a short notice. But we talked over the phone for the good part of an hour. She had mixed feelings about this marriage."

Bridget didn't know about Amy. I had never brought her up. Amy, of course, was at the wedding, resigned to what happened and keeping quiet. She had tried to dissuade me from making that decision, hammering into my head the notion that after I broke up with Jim I could make it on my own. *"You're strong… You're invincible… You're woman,"* she would sing with Helen Reddy. But I was not ready for the big fight to fulfill my destiny. Not yet. I needed some time to develop wings strong enough to fly alone. Now, I felt I was close to acquiring them, strong and magnificent and able to spread and carry me off. But where to? I was confident I'd soon find out.

"It's normal. Mothers always worry about their children. You may not understand because you don't have kids of your own, but that's the way it is. By the way, you're past thirty now, it's time to plan for a child before it's too late."

"That's what Steve says. He's been pressing me for some time. From the very beginning, actually. And I… I can't make up my mind. It'd be fun to have a little kid running around the garden. But this is a luxury I can't afford. I'd have to devote a big part of my life to him, or her, instead of pursuing my career. And I have a responsibility to myself first: to become economically independent in order not to rely on anyone, especially on my husband."

"If this is how you feel… It's sad, though. Well, I shouldn't say that. I clearly belong in another era. I cannot imagine my life without my son and the little ones."

"Don't get me wrong, I won't rule it out. But now it's not the right moment. You see, it's been only four years since I landed the position I pursued for so long, and against all odds because Steve was opposed."

"He didn't want you to go to work?"

"He didn't want me to work at this university, for sure. He was concerned people would suspect him of nepotism. But that was unfair to me. He was thinking only of himself. And so, I ignored him. There was an opening for someone with exactly my academic background in the Department of Liberal Arts, and I applied."

"And you got it. I was so proud of you when it happened."

When it happened, Bridget organized a barbeque at the farm for me and my closest friends, and Larkin treated us to the juiciest and most delicious hamburgers we had ever tasted. He also let us ride the horses, and took us on a long excursion through thick woods and steep ravines, all the way down to the river. There, we stopped, dismounted, and let the horses have a drink. "You've got to know the *real* America," he told me wiping the sweat off his neck with a red bandana, "forget about the West Coast and the East Coast. You must see and experience the rough territory in between, the land of the first settlers."

I did. I was captivated. I found myself walking through the pages of an adventure book, or a movie set.

The river is wide and placid. Our canoe floats smoothly along the banks covered with thick vegetation. The trees are so close to the edge that their roots are exposed and reach down into the water like huge writhing pythons. In a clearing is the military fort the French built in the early eighteenth century, which soon became a busy trading post. Fur trappers came all the way down from Quebec to seek commercial relations with friendly Wea Indian tribes.

The fort is a square two-story blockhouse. On the surrounding grounds, vendors and buyers exchange pelts, furniture, locks and keys, pots and pans, guns, homespun cloth, and food. People in coonskin caps, farmer garb, military uniforms, and deerhide garments and mocassins, swarm before our eyes in colorful confusion. By a campfire, women in calico dresses and bonnets sell rabbit stew and cornbread. Canoe voyagers unload their goods on the pier. It's the Feast of the Hunters' Moon, which every year in the fall brings back to life scenes from the frontier world. I look at the blockhouse. It's a good approximation of the original one. It has been rebuilt in 1930, long after the old fort fell into British hands and was subsequently destroyed by the Kentucky Militia under Federal command, in 1791. They burned it to the ground, together with neighboring Wea villages, in their fateful chase after the setting sun.

South of the fort, the river enters into a deep canyon. The banks are fifty-foot tall, overwhelming and intimidating. The water is a dense yellowish color. Our canoe is like an insect on a pond. Squinting against the sun, I look up and think I see bellicose Indian warriors posted along the ridge, led by their great chief Tecumseh, his feather headdress proudly waving in the wind. No doubt they are headed for the battlefield, determined to protect their native land from an advancing, overpowering, conquering force. The sun blinds me. I close my eyes.

When I look up again, they have disappeared.

The first drops of rain fell into my glass.

"It's raining. Quick, let's go inside." Bridget rapidly collected our stuff.

We had not noticed a huge black cloud approaching from the plains. A strong wind made the tree branches sway wildly, the flowers reclined their heads, bent over by the heavy downpour. Soon our light dresses were soaked. We ran to the shack and shut the windows. It was safe and cozy in there. Larkin did a good job repairing the roof and reinforcing the walls. He even carved some living space out of the storage room, and I furnished it with two rocking chairs bought at a yard sale, two real pieces of Americana. Bridget and I waited the storm out, finishing up the rest of the lemonade.

When I got home, Steve was watching the news, sipping a Martini. He heard me walk across the hall and called from the library.

"Honey, is it you?"

I appeared in the doorway, barefooted and with the dress glued to the skin.

"Oh, you're a mess. Go change while I fix you a drink."

"Just a glass of wine for me. No fancy stuff, thank you."

I came back after a shower.

"Come here, come sit on the couch. I hardly see you these days."

I sat in an easy chair. "Well, I'm busy with the beginning of the semester. I have to deal with red tape, prepare class materials, advise the students… It's time consuming. And then, there's my research, I must complete the papers for two conferences next month, and apply the finishing touches to my book before it goes to press."

"Are you sure it's not too much for you? Recent studies show that stress is bad for women. It makes them age prematurely."

"Perhaps this is just another lie invented by men to keep women from achieving success."

"Oh, please, spare me the feminist spiel. I hear enough of it at the office. Every day there are new demands, and new policies have to be implemented to meet them—equal rights, equal pay, equal number of faculty, equal opportunity in sports... Where's the end? It costs the university a lot of money."

"It's about time they level the playing field for women."

"Perhaps. But if we look at Affirmative Action in general, it's clear that the playing field is not being leveled. It's now tilted in the other direction. We can talk of reverse discrimination, placing well-qualified white males at a disadvantage."

I didn't have a good answer. To correct the injustice of the past with another one did not seem like 'equity.' On the other hand, I noticed that diversity on campus increased considerably from the day we arrived. The ethnic palette had gradually changed from pure white to a mix of colors. A sign that Affirmative Action had arrived even in a place like Fairville.

"Carter is falling behind in the polls." Steve had turned his attention to the news.

Most of it covered the campaigns for the oncoming presidential election in November. Carter was losing ground to his challenger, a Hollywood actor turned governor, who at first didn't seem to have much of a chance. It's difficult to unseat a president after the first term. But those two past decades had been a period of presidential instability: Kennedy was killed after only three years, Johnson completed his first term but didn't run again, Nixon had to resign two years into the second term, and Ford lost the election after serving for just two years.

Now, Carter was on shaky ground. After several gloomy years of oil shortage and high inflation, Reagan carried a message of hope and optimism, promising a brilliant economic recovery. After a number of humiliating setbacks in foreign policy, he offered the vision of an America as 'the city shining on the hill,' ready to engage and defeat the dark forces of evil. He had a grand vision, patriotic ideals, and firm conservative principles, but didn't have much of a program. His speeches were inspirational, but unrealistic. To me, they sounded high in rhetoric and short in substance. But people love to dream, and Reagan knew how to deliver his lines. Besides, he himself believed in the beautiful dream, and that made his message even more appealing.

In retrospect, he was lucky. His 'voodoo economics,' once ridiculed by George H. W. Bush, did work to a certain extent, and he was credited with an economic recovery. However, what he achieved was an illusion of prosperity, rather than solid growth. In fact, one effect of Reaganomics was the increase of the Federal budget deficit. To cover the deficit, the national debt rose from 997 billion to 2.85 trillion, changing the U.S. economic position in the world from largest international creditor to largest international debtor, and, arguably, marking the beginning of the decline of the United States as the greatest economic power.

But in foreign policy Reagan was even luckier. On the day of his inauguration, the Iranian government released the fifty-two hostages captured during the attack on the American Embassy in Tehran in '79, and held in captivity for more than one year. In the eyes of the average viewer who judges history through the television screen, Reagan became their liberator. In reality, the release had been negotiated by Carter, through the Algerian government, and a ransom was paid by releasing Iranian assets that had previously been frozen. The ransom consisted of fifty tons of gold, because the Iranians refused to accept U.S. dollars. Carter was instead remembered as a loser for a botched attempt to rescue the hostages through a military operation. Operation Eagle Claw had been carefully planned, but three helicopters encountered technical difficulties, and one was caught in a sand storm, before reaching Tehran. They crashed in the desert, and the operation was aborted. Carter was forever associated with the dramatic images of the wreckage, paraded on TV.

The other feather in Reagan's hat, at the end of his term, was the ending of the Cold War with the defeat of the 'Evil

Empire.' It is true that Reagan's rhetoric had been eloquent on this subject, and that from the height of his pulpit he uttered fiery lines against the Soviet Union, some of which have become historical idioms. However, he would not have scored better than his predecessors if it were not for fortunate external circumstances. First of all, the Soviet Union was on the verge of economic collapse, as the old centralized system was no longer sustainable. Secondly, a younger leader emerged, who understood the situation and sought to reform the system. Without Gorbachev, who came of age in the years of reforms and 'cultural liberalization' under Khrushchev, the transition to the market economy and a quasi-democratic government would not have been possible.

However, one of Reagan's achievements is undeniable. He restored the sense of patriotism in the majority of the population and revived the love of country that was lost in the previous two turbulent decades.

Reagan was being interviewed on CBS.

"Finally, someone who makes sense," Steve said. "This guy really lifts up my spirit. What a difference. Carter seems to carry his 'malaise speech' into everything he says. I get depressed every time I hear him speak. And the worst thing of all is that silly broad smile of his... How many teeth does he have? Sixty-four?"

"Alright, you don't like Carter's policies. But do you have to get so personal? I feel sorry for the man. He came in with good intentions, and has honestly been working for the good of the country. Besides, he never used the word 'malaise,' somehow it got stuck to him."

"Ah, women... They have such a tender heart. You may be a good teacher, but you'll never make a good president. Don't you realize that he is responsible for the current situation in Iran? That he undermined the shah's government and facilitated the return of Khomeini from his exile in Paris? You just don't get it. What we need now is a strong leader. Not someone who turns everything he touches into a fiasco."

"You're making strange assumptions about women. For one, I'm quite capable of making bold decisions. And then... —the news shifted to the daily report on the hostage crisis— look at those thugs, those religious fanatics and their Islamic revolution. I'm furious with them. That black-clad figure of doom of their ayatollah gives me the creeps. Every evening we have to endure the images of our guys, blindfolded and handcuffed. I'm absolutely in favor of a decisive response. Perhaps Carter miscalculated at the beginning, but then he did try to mount a military operation to resolve the crisis, and I'm sure he'll try again."

"In this case, he must be quick because after November 4th he'll be gone."

Walter Cronkite wrapped up the evening news. He reminded us, as he did every night adding one day to the count, that it was day #314 of the hostage captivity.

Dorothy called us to dinner.

Stella's Story: Chapter 13
Fairville, 1984-1985

The road was straight and smooth, cutting the flat land into two equal halves. Field patches of different color, a farm, a line of trees, horses behind a white fence, a miniature church, occasional hand-made signs advertising a fruit and vegetable market glided by the car on both sides. The perfectly shaped disk of an autumnal sun was pinned to an incredibly blue sky. Everything was neatly arranged, like in a children's coloring book. The simple beauty of the landscape spoke of hard labor, basic values, and good will, qualities that distinguished the local folks. Qualities that they inherited from those who first ventured into this territory. On this side, it was quite different from the untamed area along the river. It was hard to believe that out of so much violence the settlers created so much harmony. *Country road, take me home…* It would have been a good sound track to the picture. But this road did not take me home. I was a stranger, a guest.

A few more miles and a short stretch across an empty lot, and I reached my destination.

On the edge of a huge cornfield, a big tent had been set up for the kick off of a new venture, a plant for the production of ethanol. A large number of people were already inside. Many more were slowly moving in. I got in line. We were greeted at the door by the company mascot in a corncob costume, and each of us received a bag of popcorn with the logo of the corporation.

All seats close to the podium were taken. With popcorn in hand, I took a seat in the back. The place was crowded. We were the stockholders, the first batch of people willing to risk their hard-earned dollars to be part of a project that, we believed, would revolutionize the energy industry and terminate U.S. oil dependency on the Middle East. Our motivation had a patriotic component, although we all hoped for a large pot of gold down the road.

"Nothing will come of it," Steve said when a broker approached us. "The country is not ready, there's no infrastructure to sustain such a venture." But I insisted. "Do as you want," he then said. "But with your own money. I won't put a penny into this absurd enterprise."

I ended up investing two thousand dollars. It was quite a substantial sum for me, although I had more money to spend now. I got tenure the previous year, and with it, a salary increase. First thing I did, on the occasion of a professional convention in New York, was to splurge on a gorgeous full-length designer coat lined, hood and all, with thick red fox. I justified it to myself with the excuse that winters in Fairville were Siberian cold.

But ethanol was my first investment. A thrilling experience.

I looked around. There were some people from the university, but the rest were farmers and folks from neighboring towns. They locked their barns, their grocery stores on Main Street, put the CLOSED sign on the law firm's glass door, secured the entrance to the city paper office, and came to the meeting. I felt very proud of being one of the co-owners of the corporation.

The president came to the podium and unveiled some graphics and charts. I was engrossed in the presentation. A man came in late and sat next to me, in one of the few empty seats. How annoying. I hate when people are late for a show. God forbid he starts talking to me. I kept looking straight ahead, ignoring his presence.

"Hi."

I looked at him.

"Hi, Nik! What are you doing here?"

"Practicing capitalism." He laughed under a smart mustache that tracked down into a neatly trimmed beard. His soft curly hair matched the beard's dark golden tones.

It was Nikolay Vozbudin, a colleague who had recently joined the faculty. He was Russian and wrote his name as Nik, pronounced *Neek*. He took advantage of a window of opportunity that opened up in the Soviet Union in the mid-seventies for those who applied for emigration. Most of them were Jews. But there were also non-Jewish intellectuals like Nik, outspoken and independent-minded, that the regime viewed as a threat and was happy to get rid of. He was renowned internationally in the fields of semiotics and literary theory, but at home he was not allowed to pursue his research and publish his works. They were of the wrong kind. They were branded as being 'formalistic' and not in line with the official rules that the State applied to all creative endeavors, the so-called doctrine of Socialist Realism. Nevertheless, his studies were smuggled to the West over the years by visiting scholars, and published abroad. When he arrived in the U.S., he was sort of a celebrity in academic circles.

I attended some of his lectures and chatted with him superficially at faculty meetings, but I was too busy with my work and I didn't seek to deepen the acquaintance. Although I noticed that he was attractive. Very attractive. And perhaps this was why I kept at a distance.

Now we were very close in that crowded space. Our elbows touched, and he leaned over to talk. His face was just inches from mine.

"You know what goes well with popcorn?" he asked when the presentation was over.

I shook my head. No.

"Vodka."

"That's a bizarre combination. Usually one thinks of vodka and caviar."

"That if you want to be traditional." He locked eyes with me. "Come over to my place, my refrigerator is well stocked. We can be traditional, innovative, or something else…"

How daring of him. After all, we hardly knew each other, and I was a married woman. He must have known that. Later, when I got to know him better, I realized that for a Russian man those were negligible details.

His blatant disregard for social norms, his naked intentions, and the raw desire in his eyes were contagious.

I silently turned around and started inching my way toward the exit. He kept close to me. We were squeezed together in the crowd. When we reached the door, he placed a hand on the nape of my neck. It was hot. A high-tension shock went down my spine.

"I'll be waiting for you," he said before removing the hand.

Then, he strode away.

The wait wasn't long.

He yanked the door open before I had the time to knock. He grabbed my hand in midair and without a word, abruptly, pulled me into his arms. Our kiss was long and passionate.

He ripped off my clothes. "Beautiful!" He stared at my body, entranced. It was not a compliment addressed to me. It was the expression of an intense visual pleasure, a private emotion of his own.

He had set the food on the coffee table in front of a large, square couch that was also his bed. The lights were dimmed, and Glazunov's *Saxophone Concerto* floated around the room softening every sharp angle with an erotic caress.

That night, I learned how to drink vodka *do dna*, bottoms up, how to spread a thin layer of butter on a piece of toast and top it with a thick layer of caviar, then sink my teeth into it and take a big morsel, and twirl it around the mouth to savor every grain of that saline delight.

"This is not just food. This is ecstasy…" Nik said, licking my lips to pick up a few residual grains.

We completely forgot about popcorn.

That night, I also learned how to make love in a new way, refined and hedonistic, artistically crafted to enhance every sense, an erotic game aimed to remove all inhibitions and release the most basic instincts.

I left at dawn. The sun was slowly applying a faint pink stroke to the sky. My thoughts were the same color. I felt a strange euphoria for the new day, an intense happiness of being alive.

Steve was away on business. Nobody was waiting for me. I drove slowly, with the window down, savoring the smells and colors of a glorious morning.

When I passed by Bridget's house, she was already out in the yard, raking dry leaves and gathering them in big, neat piles. She paused and looked at me, surprised, a question in her eyes. I waved and kept going. I had nothing to share with her. Dear good Bridget would not have understood.

After that first night, Nik's house became my inevitable destination at the end of the workday, as if, no matter where I was, all streets converged there in a swirl and I was sucked in by a strong current.

Our encounters were brief. We could rarely spend the night together. I had to be home for dinner.

Fortunately, dinner for us was late because Steve liked to spend a couple of hours at the club for drinks. After dinner, I often had an excuse for not sleeping with him, I have to get up early in the morning, I have work to do tonight, I don't feel well… He too was tired, or had a drink too many, and usually did not insist.

But, one winter night I could no longer pretend. Steve's presence, his voice, his looks, his manners, everything about him had become intolerable. I couldn't stand his touch. I could not respond to his niceties, his little kisses, his surges of desire. I didn't even care to react to his insensitive quips meant to put a woman in her place.

I knew that I didn't love him when we got married, although I appreciated his qualities and thought that love might come later. But now, I felt a physical dislike for him. Another man crawled into my veins, touched my nerves and saturated my brain.

"The storm's already started," Steve said pulling down the drapes on the magic spectacle of the snowy yard. "The forecast is for two feet of snow tonight."

"Wonderful!"

"Nothing wonderful when you've to shovel it in the morning." The fireplace filled the room with its reassuring crackling and glowing. He took my hand and pulled me up from the couch. "Come, let's go to bed early. It's a night to keep cozy and warm together."

"I can't. I'm sorry."

"You can't… what?"

"I can't make love to you."

"Since when?"

"It's been a while."

"But you did, recently."

"I did because I wanted to please you, but I didn't feel like it. And now, I can't."

"Is there another man?'

"Yes."

He paused. Then he looked sternly into my eyes. "Look. You don't have to say any more. I don't even want to know who he is. Just tell me that it's over. Tell me that you won't see him again, and I will pardon you."

"You don't understand. I'm in love with him."

Now he was mad. "You're a fool. You have a position, a house, a husband. You have responsibilities. You can't throw it all out in a moment of insanity. I won't let you ruin my reputation."

"Sorry, I can't help it."

I stepped into the hall and reached for my 'Siberian' coat.

"Wait! You're making a big mistake."

But I was already on the threshold, the wind whistling in my ears. I faded out in a whirl of snowflakes.

Swish-swish, swish-swish. The windshield wipers kept going at an accelerated pace, clearing a crescent of dubious visibility in the mass of snow that clung to the car. They kept the pace with my heart-beat, *boom-boom, swish-swish.* Why did my heart beat so fast? It was not fear. Although, several inches had already accumulated on the road and I could hardly see anything. The headlights bounced against a white wall that they could not penetrate. Behind me, the lights of the house on the hill were no longer visible.

Boom-boom, swish-swish. It was not fear. It was anticipation, desire, obsession, madness, delirium, all the emotions poets associate with the irrational force euphemistically called love. Like Barbra Streisand, I was *a woman in love,* and *I'd do anything/To get you into my world/And hold you within/It's a right I defend...*

No cars were out that night. The roads had been erased under a thick blanket that leveled everything. But I knew the way. I could find it even in the dark. Two more turns, then a long stretch, then the cul-de-sac, and there, at the edge of the woods, his house, a cabin, really, no more than a cabin. *But why is it dark?* No lights inside. *He's not home? No, no, it can't be...*

I got out of the car. I wanted to run up to the door and knock and knock. But the snow was deep on the trail and the long coat impeded my movements. Anxiety was chocking me. I took a deep breath, and the snow filled my mouth. I pulled up the hood and buried my face in the fox lining, to no avail. The snow filled my eyes, I could hardly see. A few more steps, a few more steps...

And then, by the gate, a tall figure began to take shape, dark against the white landscape, firm against the raging elements. I collapsed in his arms.

"I knew you would come. I felt your energy reaching out to me."

"I thought you weren't home. I was desperate. I would not have survived. What were you doing outside in the dark?"

"I was waiting for you. This night is for us, tempestuous and magnificent, and perilous. Like a *burya*."

The wind blew off my hood and disheveled my hair. Icy snowflakes hit my face like a swarm of pins.

He picked me up and carried me inside.

When we woke up in the middle of the night, the storm had subsided.

"D'you feel better?" he asked.

"Much better. I feel like I've survived two storms. You were even wilder than the storm outside."

"I know I'm intense. But you're a passionate woman. You respond to me, and your sensitivity is exciting. I feel you deeply."

"We feel each other. And we are well attuned."

It was dark in the room. The only light came from the fireplace, but even that was about to go out. Nik got up from the couch and put a few logs on the embers. Suddenly, long flames shot up, hissing like fiery snakes. Nik stirred the fire with a poker, naked against the sparking background, like a Greek god forging a spear.

"Turn on the light, please. I have to go pee."

"There is no light. We lost power in the middle of the storm."

"Oh, that's why the house looked dark and empty from outside."

"I was looking for candles when I saw your headlights approaching. I immediately knew it was you."

"D'you believe in ESP?"

"It's not a matter of believing, it's a matter of sensing. In this case, I picked up the waves you released. The human body is an excellent conductor of electricity."

"We certainly did a better job than the utility company."

"For sure. However, now we're trivializing the matter. Better to leave it in the realm of poetry, where physical phenomena are transformed into powerful emotions, irresistible drives, blind passions, delirious thoughts, unleashed desires, erotic dreams... We love novels because they convey all this."

"Yes, good novels can leave a mark on our imagination. Certainly, Tolstoy didn't write about electricity and wave lengths when he described the encounter of Anna Karenina and Vronsky in a small train station on the way to St. Petersburg in a boisterous winter night. He wrote of a 'blustering storm' and its 'awfulness and beauty,' as metaphors for Anna's emotions."

"Let's have a literary discussion some other time. Here's a candle for you. Careful not to trip."

The bathroom was just a few steps away, in the hallway. But the narrow circle of light around me seemed to dilate the invisible space and extend the distance into the dark.

I put down the candle by the sink and sat on the toilet. Nik emerged from the hallway into the radius of the candlelight. He crouched down in front of me, and our eyes interlocked. He cupped one hand and slipped it between my thighs. "Pee in my hand. Do it." It was a command, but a soft one, as I had already responded to his touch rather than his voice.

Afterward, he picked me up and sat me on his lap, my legs around his body. He took me right there, on the bare floor.

* * *

"I made tea, real Russian *chai,* dark and fragrant." Nik put down the tray on the coffee table. He poured me a cup and joined me under the duvet. "This'll keep you warm. The fireplace alone is not enough."

"Hum, excellent! Where d'you get real Russian *chai* in this all-American town?"

"I get it from Russia. Lyuba packs my favorite brand, and whatever American friends happen to be there bring it to the States and mail it to me."

"Who's Lyuba?"

"My wife."

"Your wife?! And you left her behind?! Or, was it her decision?"

"She wanted to come but she couldn't. The authorities refused her an exit visa."

"Why?"

"Who knows why? There's nothing rational in this kind of decisions. They found some excuses: missing papers, the application was filed with the wrong office, she did not show up for a hearing... all false. It was pure harassment. They gave me one week to pack and leave."

"Oh, that's awful. I suppose it was a one-way visa for you."

"That's right. I can't go back. They stripped me of my Soviet citizenship and took my passport away."

"She must feel terrible there, without knowing whether she will ever see you again."

"I know, it's hard for her. But like most Russian women she has great tolerance for suffering. And she's very devoted to me. She loves me deeply and unconditionally, I am her *raison d'être.* Even if I am far away."

"I don't get it. Something's not right. You have a life here, you're successful professionally. And also in your private life you're doing pretty well, I must say... But what about her?"

"It may sound odd, but the truth is that love sustains her

and makes her happy in a strange way. You don't understand because you're a western woman. You don't have that sense of abnegation that is deeply ingrained in a Russian woman's heart. It's in our culture, you know? There are hundreds of stories, in our great literature or in history books, of devoted wives who leave everything behind to follow their husbands all the way to Siberia, on foot, with the convict convoy. And they do it because they believe that love will save their men."

"This is admirable, but it's not your case. I don't think there's any need for Lyuba to save you. You should free her from that burden. She has a right to live her life freely."

"You want me to ask her not to love me? This would be a terrible blow to her. As for the right to live freely, you don't know what you're talking about. There are no rights in the Soviet Union. Human rights and civil rights are a farce, not to speak of women's rights. They are all guaranteed under the law, but are constantly violated. Our Constitution is only window dressing. The State gives rights, the State can take them away."

I put down my empty cup and snuggled up to his warm body.

"Does she live all by herself?"

"She lives with my mother, who has a large apartment in one of those stately skyscrapers dating back to Stalin's time. My father was a physicist and a distinguished member of the Academy of Sciences, and we enjoyed all the privileges of the regime. When he died, mother was allowed to keep the apartment. The State may be a generous patron if you're lucky, or it may crush you like a bug if you're among the unlucky ones."

"D'you have children?"

"Not by her."

"What d'you mean?"

"I have two sons, but they live with their mothers. I didn't see much of them. They're okay. Single mothers get state subsidies, they don't need me."

"I find it hard to believe. Why didn't you have children with Lyuba?"

"I don't know. They just didn't come."

"Does she have a job?"

"Of course. In the Soviet Union it's mandatory to have a job. Unemployed people may even be jailed on charges of 'hooliganism.' She's a librarian in a state archive."

"Sounds sort of depressing."

"Everything that's state controlled is depressing. And that includes all individual activities in public life—at work, in the street, at the theater, at the restaurant, on the bus, in the park, at the museum, at school... everywhere. Behavior and speech should fall within certain parameters in order to keep out of trouble. The citizen is constantly under surveillance, one way or the other. The state police informers are everywhere. Even a false accusation may ruin your life."

"What do people do for fun?"

"In the private sphere, things are different. Among family and friends, the ordinary folks can be themselves and enjoy the small pleasures they can afford. In the intellectual circles, by reaction to conformism in public life, we party wildly and have the most intense and unrestrained sex life. Many creative people—writers, artists, musicians, film directors, art and literary critics—challenge the State and seek alternative spaces to express themselves. Every night we have extravagant gatherings at a poet's apartment, or an artist's studio, or an actor's dacha. Those are meetings of the minds and a triumph of the senses. At the bottom of that carnival, however, there is a sense of despair, a feeling of doom. The atmosphere is decadent. We know that we have no future. Some drink themselves to death. Others, like me, look for a chance to emigrate."

"And this kind of behavior is allowed?!"

"The KGB give us a long leash, provided that those activities are confined to the dens of the intellectual elite and won't become public and create a scandal. But they are ready to rein us in at any moment if they feel openly threatened."

Nik was no longer with me under the duvet, in the safe intimacy of his cabin. His voice seemed to come from far away, carrying a deep pain and wistful nostalgia.

"You speak in the present tense, as if you were still there."

"Nothing changed since I left five years ago. One leader dies, another takes his place. They're each other's clones, selected by a handful of men, the members of the Politburo, who together are the power. And they hide behind an alluring lie, calling the power 'the dictatorship of the proletariat,' as if it belonged to the people, while the people have always been trampled upon. True, at the beginning many believed in the alluring lie, in the collective effort to build a just and prosperous future for all. Instead, the power enslaved the people, made them dependent on the State for their needs, provided the bare necessities and demanded the utmost subservience, dispensed privileges to political allies and murdered opponents with equal ease, and stripped every citizen of his dignity by suppressing individual initiative and freedom of expression."

"D'you see any possibility of change?"

"I don't. This newly-appointed leader, Mikhail Gorbachev, who wants to reform the economy and liberalize society, will not last long. To be under the thumb of a strong ruler is the destiny of Russia. Just look at her history. Frankly, I think that our people would be terribly confused if Russia were to become a democracy. They wouldn't know how to cope with freedom. Too many responsibilities, you know?"

"How are you coping with democracy here?"

"I adjusted very quickly. But one thing is to adjust to a mature democratic system, and another is to build that system in a country that has never had democratic institutions. I love my country, and I will forever live with a sense of pain for her sad predicament. But, as a good immigrant, I am learning the

American way. I even bought shares of the ethanol company and developed a taste for popcorn."

"Now you're being ironic."

"Perhaps, but I'm serious about the fundamental American values based on the respect for the individual. The idea of placing freedom *from* the government at the center of the constitutional order was a stroke of genius."

"I agree." The conversation I had with Worthington some twenty years ago came back to mind vividly. "But something happened in the sixties, when leftist movements started challenging the system and advocating a Marxist revolution."

"They were able to do so precisely because they lived in a democracy. In the Soviet Union, protest and dissent are not possible. Protect your system. Beware of anyone who claims that he acts for the people, who talks of redistributing wealth, of making everyone equal. You fall in the trap and you end up on the 'Animal Farm.' Believe me, I've been there."

I poured myself another cup of tea and leaned back against the pillows. Our bodies no longer touched.

"In any case, something good came out of those protests. Minorities got rights, including women. The feminist movement has been very effective," I said.

"It had the effect of turning women into men-haters. They've got their rights and I'm happy for that, but they've also been indoctrinated. Now the feminists are a political organization with an ideology, a doctrine, and forms of speech and behavior that they want to impose on everyone. What was at the beginning a liberation movement has become tyrannical. The concept of 'rights' has been stretched into absurdity and has become synonymous with 'privilege' or 'entitlement.' This is the normal pattern of all leftist movements that start with the goal of liberating this or that group. They end up imposing on society the tyranny of the minority. It's an insidious process that will erode the fabric of this country over time if the people are not alert."

"I thought of myself as a feminist when I went marching for the ERA back in the seventies with thousands of women, all dressed in white, all hopeful that the Amendment would pass and would symbolically mark the beginning of a better world. I never thought of myself as a men-hater."

"Did you ever love a man?"

"What d'you mean?"

"You don't love your husband, and you don't love me. Did you ever love a man?"

"Yes, I did."

"And why are you not with him?"

"I'm not sure. I can't explain it. Gradually we fell apart, and then an incident triggered the inevitable outcome, and we were no longer together."

"Did he leave you?"

"No, I did. I guess this is the greatest sin in the eyes of a Russian man."

"True, but ours is a patriarchal society, very much male-oriented. Therefore, I'm conditioned to expect from a woman complete devotion. Here, it's a different story. Have you heard from him?"

"No. But I know he's doing well. He is a successful author now. He wrote the scripts for the best films that came out of Hollywood in recent years."

"D'you miss him?"

Do I miss him? Yes… No… No, no, I don't want to think about it. "Never look back, look forward," Amy says.

"It's been a long time. My life is different now."

"I take the answer is, yes… Well, go to sleep now. Tomorrow we'll have to dig out your car."

We were not able to dig out my car, and the streets were impassable. We had to wait for the snow removal service, which arrived three days later. In the meantime, we had to live without electricity, relying on the gas stove for hot water and cooking. But there wasn't much food in the house besides caviar and tea.

A feeling of entrapment crept in and made me uneasy. Nik got on my nerves. At the end of the third day, I was anxious to leave. "Good bye." "Should I expect you tomorrow?" "No, not tomorrow." "The day after?" "Perhaps, give me some time." "Are you tired of me?" "Don't ask so many questions." "I'll be waiting for you." "Bye."

Steve and I lived in the Tudor house like two roommates. The house was large enough to allow us to have separate quarters. He did not want a scandal to break out and possibly jeopardize his career. We still had dinner together when we were home, and our conversation at the table was civil but cold.

I kept seeing Nik, from time to time, but the flame was dying out. I had to move on, to leave behind the comfort of that provincial little niche and confront the wide wild world. Amy was pushing, "What are you waiting for? Soon you'll be forty, d'you want to spend the rest of your life in the boonies? Now you're still in time, in a few years it may be too late. Take your chance, go and live your life."

And yet, it wasn't easy. Once again I was going to turn the page, to leave behind my past… like I did when I left Italy… like I did when I left LA. This time, I didn't have a good reason, I was just responding to an undefined urge for growth, for self-fulfillment. "How American!" Amy was telling me. "How foolish!" Bridget was telling me.

Bridget didn't understand my predicament. To her, I lived in the best of all worlds. She didn't understand my refusal to have a family, or my relationship with Nik. She saw, however, that I felt restless, and she tried to compensate with love. She was there for me, always, with lemonade, apple pie, and a good word.

Life was good and easy in Fairville. The past ten years had been a period of healing for the country, and of consolidation of the concessions obtained during the time of turmoil on campuses and across the nation. With the end of the Vietnam war, order was restored. No more fear of being drafted, no more rallies, no more sit-ins. The country was so eager to forget about that tragic experience that gave the cold shoulder to the veterans coming home from the battlefields. Disabled in body and mind, the returning soldiers were treated with hostility, disdain or, at best, indifference. As if punishing them would alleviate the collective sense of shame the nation experienced for an unpopular war which ended in defeat. The protesters of yesterday have gradually been reabsorbed into the mainstream. Here in Fairville the greatest excitement was the football game, when the university team played at home and the big stadium was overflowing with thousands of chanting fans. Occasional brawls over scores replaced political riots. On weekdays, from the vantage point of the faculty club terrace, one could see students going to class, coming from class, playing frisbee, heading for the track and field, the tennis courts, the pool, and lying on the lawn to get the first tan of the summer or catch the last sunrays in the fall.

"This picture is so different from the way it was twenty years ago. You know, unrest, confrontation, open rebellion. It's as if all that didn't leave a mark."

"At least not on the surface. But don't fool yourself, there may be underground forces you cannot see," Elliot sneered.

We were on the faculty club terrace, sipping beer and observing the activities on the ground. Elliot was a professor of English and a poet. He was also openly gay, a thing that in those days, and especially in Fairville, was talked about with caution, as something to be tolerated but implicitly rejected. Or, it was addressed with exaggerated acceptance—see how liberal and open-minded we are. As a consequence, Elliot didn't have many friends, although he was respected for his poetry that won him a few prestigious awards. I enjoyed his company, and we often met between classes and embarked in long philosophical conversations. He was in his late-fifties, had a big head of grey curly hair, long and unkempt, and a bushy beard. He didn't clean up, unlike most of his contemporaries.

"How did it all begin back then? You know, when I arrived, the 'revolution' was already unfolding. What was there in the beginning?"

"In the beginning was the Word. Literally. It didn't begin with the Flower Children, it began with the poets. I was a student at Columbia University in the mid-forties, and there I met them all: Ginsberg, Burroughs, Kerouac, Carr, the kernel of the Beat Generation. We wrote, we read to each other, we had public readings... We wanted to change the world with the power of the word. We wanted to inject a shot of spirituality into a stagnant society awash in material possessions. Our philosophy was counterculture and anti-materialistic."

Elliot took a big swallow of beer, staring blankly ahead.

"And then what happened? Come on, I want to hear it from someone who was actually there."

"We were 'on the road' a lot..."

"Pun intended?"

"What d'you think? We moved to San Francisco and joined the poets of the Renaissance. We performed at the Six Gallery reading with Rexroth, Ferlinghetti and the others. What a great time. Our movement finally hit the public consciousness. Then in the late fifties we were back in New York and settled in the Village, and that became a hub for the best creative minds, not just poets. In the evening we'd gather at the San Remo, or at Minetta Tavern, and here the door opens and Pollock enters, or deKooning, or Kline... Often the cafés were too small to contain us and we spilled out onto Washington

Square. There were big crowds, jazz concerts, readings, discussions."

"You make it sound like a big happy kermes, but there was also a dark side to the beat movement. The public was uncomfortable with drug use, alcohol, and homosexual relations graphically described by many of you."

"Those were vehicles in our search for truth. Ours was a spiritual movement. Kerouac believed that the holy man must sweat for God. He was profoundly Catholic, and later was attracted to Buddhism. Many of us were. We introduced Asian religions to the West. Our goal was to develop and improve the inner self. It was the media that called us beatniks with a pejorative connotation. We never used that name, we were the Beats."

"Really? And what's the difference?"

Elliot got up, threw the beer can into the trash bin, lit up a cigarette, and hunched over, resting his elbows on the railway. He took a long drag, looking out beyond the tree-tops.

"Big difference. Kerouac came up with the name Beat Generation early on, taking the word 'beat' from underworld slang. Among the hustlers and drug addicts in the Village it meant 'downtrodden'. But he expanded and enriched its meaning, giving it a spiritual connotation. He lifted the word from the street corners of the inner city to identify a generation of visionary bums, 'beautiful in an ugly graceful new way,' as he put it."

"And where does 'beatnik' come from?"

"That is a media stereotype appropriated by market forces. All of a sudden it was cool to be beatnik, and under that label small shops and large chain stores offered to middle-class America black turtlenecks, French berets and dark glasses that gave the philistine in disguise a sense of thrilling transgression. 'Beatnik' was coopted by that voracious consumer society we had struggled against."

"Yet, some essential features migrated into the counterculture of the sixties. The Beats faded out and the hippies faded in. They shared the same attraction to Eastern philosophies and the use of drugs. And they also rejected the establishment."

"With them, those were superficial features. No substance. The hippies thumbed their nose at society and called themselves rebels in order to live in an eternal carnival. Kerouac saw through it. He denounced them for lacking conviction and criticized their political protests as an excuse to get hyped. He even split with Ginsberg on that, because Ginsberg embraced the hippie movement and became an active participant in anti-war demonstrations. The Beats never engaged in politics, that was below our calling."

"Another difference I can see is that hippie creativity expressed itself in music rather than poetry, although some of their lyrics were poetic."

"Poetic in a folksy way. That's why their songs became so popular. Poetry is not for the masses. They gathered in Laurel Canyon, in Frank Zappa's big house that they called Log Cabin to give it a 'natural' flavor, children of the fat bourgeoisie, many coming from military families while their dads were commanding operations in Nam, lived communally and made music."

"I know. All the big bands were formed there—the Byrds, The Mamas and the Papas, the Doors… you name it. They had a knack for catching the spirit of the time and creating a new music style, rock music. You must give them that."

"Of course, their music was instrumental in spreading the hippie culture. Hordes of teenagers moved west lured by those 'pied pipers': come to San Francisco, put a flower in your hair, you know… They came, not only from the States, but from Europe as well, and the youth counterculture was born."

"Yes, and the LSD combined with music certainly helped create the magic atmosphere."

"Psychedelic concerts became the norm. The Monterey Pop Festival was the first rock concert that originated all the others. It was big. It lasted three days, a creature of 'Papa' John Phillips. He proved himself to be a great impresario. Nobody had ever produced anything like that. It was in '67, I think."

"Precisely. I arrived in Venice a few months later, in the early fall, and those who attended were still talking about it."

"Tens of thousands gathered on the County Fairgrounds on that occasion, and the festival got unprecedented media coverage. For the first time mainstream America was exposed to the look and sound of the hippie culture that was going to change the world as we knew it. Future international stars made their debut performance there. Jimi Hendrix, for one. And Janis Joplin, Otis Redding, the Who, and... so many. After that, the center of the music industry moved from New York to Los Angeles. Even Bob Dylan's songs, which were born in Greenwich Village in the early sixties, the first songs of social protest, migrated to the West Coast and were assimilated into the hippie culture."

Elliot put out the cigarette and flicked the butt over. He turned and leaned against the railing.

"Were you there for the Summer of Love?" I asked.

"In Haight-Ashbury? No, that was a gathering of adolescents. I mean, adolescents of all ages, mostly college students and dropouts, but also some middle-class people bored with their daily routine, looking for alternative lifestyles, communal living and psychedelic trips. It was a phenomenon of huge proportions. As many as one hundred thousand converged there after Monterey. They jammed in bunches into those large Victorian apartments in the Haight and got stoned. There, everything was free: free housing, free food, free love... No need to work, no need for money, a Council provided for all the necessities, including medical care. The media gave it incessant coverage, and the gathering was copycatted in other countries, causing alarm among the population. But by the end of the summer, things deteriorated, the district was over-crowded, many went hungry and slept in the parks, there were also drug problems."

"That's why they disbanded and came down to LA?"

"Some went back to school. For them it had been just a vacation. Others drifted away to communes or to southern beaches. And those who remained in the neighborhood declared the 'death of the hippie' in a mock funeral announcement. They did it to stop the influx of new people and encourage their followers to stay put and spread the 'revolution' at home."

"And it worked. Everywhere, the hippies created a generation gap that did not exist before. They replaced Puritan ethic with the pursuit of pleasure. The teenagers took over the adult world."

"The feast went on for another couple of years. Ken Kesey traveled around the country on his graffiti-covered bus, offering acid to the kids like an ice-cream vendor, with the effect of sending them over to 'the cuckoo's nest'."

"At the time of the legendary Woodstock festival the revolution was still bubbling."

"Yes, but Woodstock was also its swan song. Dozens of musicians, the most popular bands, five hundred thousand people—some say, one million—music, pot, and love 'round the clock. And, amazingly, everything went smoothly, no incidents, no violence. A perfect love-in... Excuse me, I need another beer."

He came back with two cans.

"No, thanks. I still got some."

He sat next to me and put his feet up on the railing.

"Why did you say Woodstock was a swan song?"

"Because it was. A few months later a replica was organized in Altamont near San Francisco. But there, things took the wrong turn. The Hells Angels were in charge of security and didn't do a good job. A girl was stabbed and killed, not an innocent victim because she drew a gun when the Rolling Stones were performing on stage… but still. Then, violence broke out and four more people died. That event tarnished the hippie image in the eyes of many people, even those who sympathized with the movement."

"In addition, it was precisely at that time that the 'Manson family' murders occurred, and the public associated Manson with the hippies."

"That was a gross distortion because he was very marginal. He had music ambitions and hung out with Dennis Wilson and Terry Melcher for a while. But, as his trial revealed, he was mainly a psychopath, a bloody criminal. In any case, as the flowers were on the wane, the guns came in full force. Violence on campuses erupted, guerrilla formations emerged, militant groups attacked their targets. Every day we learned a new name: the Weathermen, Black Panthers, Black Power, the Symbionese Liberation Army…"

"Oh, yes, the unfortunate case of Patty Hearst. Great stuff for a novel, the kidnapped heiress turned terrorist, and the dramatic end of her comrades in the flames of their burning safe house during a shootout with the police. I remember watching the live report on TV. It was never ascertained who put the house on fire. In any case, Patty wasn't there, and later she served jail time."

"For a short term. And when she came out it was all forgotten. Terrorism went underground and some were arrested and convicted. People had other things to worry about: inflation, the oil shortage, the Watergate…

"So, the hippie movement imploded?"

"Yes. But something of it remained. Some features were co-opted into mainstream culture. Like Yoga and pot. And now, we pretend to live 'in perfect harmony' while drinking Coca-Cola. At the same time, those terrorists who have served their term are gradually being released into society. I heard they're getting teaching positions in some big universities.

Don't ask me why, it's beyond my comprehension. It's like letting the fox into the chicken coop."

Life was good and easy in Fairville. Idyllic, I'd say. So much so, that I took advantage of any possible occasion to escape. I often traveled to this or that conference, symposium, convention, or the like. For professional reasons, of course, but also in search of excitement.

I traveled a lot. A conference in New Orleans, a convention in Boston, a lecture in Denver, a symposium in New York, a seminar in Seattle, and occasional engagements in Europe.

When I was on that side of the ocean, I often included a trip home. Mother was still young-looking and beautiful. Our bond remained strong, and every time we met it was like we had never parted. Over the years we kept an intense correspondence, one letter a week, and she even came to visit three or four times. At home things had changed, Villa Flora was no longer the same. After *signora* Amelia died, the house remained opened only for a few months in the summer. Recently, it had begun to show signs of neglect. Humidity was attacking the frescoes on the walls and ceilings, the mosaic floors were missing a few pieces, and the flowerbeds in the garden were overgrown with weeds. It was no longer the shining place of my youth, the fairy-tale castle of my childhood. Amy shared my feelings, but kept reminding me, "Never mind, our life is in America." Mother never encouraged me to move back home. She, too, thought that I had better opportunities in America and that, since I made my choice twenty years ago, I should stick to it.

My absences were frequent but brief. In between, I kept up with the demands of my job and spent some pleasant hours with Nik in the cabin by the woods. I also enjoyed the company of a group of bright and vibrant faculty women. We worked together and we had fun together. At the end of the day, we'd go for a work out at the gym, where we took turns acting as each other's trainer. *Let's get physical, physical/Let me hear your body talk, your body talk/Let me hear your body talk...* We took Olivia Newton-John's exhortation seriously. Then, after a relaxing sauna, we'd go for a bite to eat at Pete's Diner, a funky little place that maintained the charm of its better days.

Sitting in a booth upholstered in red plastic, we were being treated to jumbo hot dogs and vanilla milkshake.

"Tonight I'm gonna have a second milkshake. I deserve it. I lost ten pounds in a week." Michèle was over forty and in a better shape than her teenage daughter. She came from France, after her husband divorced her and ran away with his secretary.

"I'll take credit for that. You must admit I'm a good trainer. I really made you sweat." Martha was tall and strong. At forty-five she was the eldest among us. She had three grown-up sons and a retired husband who cultivated orchids in their green house.

"No, I think it was Kelly's aerobics that did the trick. Actually, it worked for all of us." Lauren had a nicely shaped figure with all the curves in the right places. Kelly had the body of a dancer, flexible and resilient.

"Girls, let's celebrate the fact that we all have a Wonder-Woman body. Today I broke the record of one-hundred sit-ups on a bench propped up at a 45° angle. Now, what's next?" That was me speaking.

Kelly: "What d'you mean, what's next? D'you have something in mind?"

"No, nothing in particular. It was a philosophical question. What d'you wanna do with your life?"

Martha: "I'll take early retirement, leave my husband with his orchids, and go study the whales in Alaska."

"No… seriously."

Kelly: "I'll write the ultimate book on the semiotics of aerobic movements in postmodern body communication. How 'bout that? D'you think it'll get me a promotion?"

Lauren: "No. It's not outrageous enough. To be noted you must write something so esoteric that nobody can understand it. So the reviewers can say that it's the work of a genius and no one would dare contradict them. Just like it happens with abstract art in most cases."

Kelly: "Don't worry, I'll push it over the line. And what about you? What d'you wanna do with your life?"

Lauren: "I'll apply for a job as a Playboy Bunny. I'll put my brain to rest and my curves to use."

Two young guys passed by our booth on their way out.

"Hi, professor! Enjoy your dinner," one said greeting Lauren with a smirk.

Lauren (in a whisper): "Oh, shit! He's a student of mine. D'you think he heard me say that?"

Kelly: "He may. And he may even appreciate the fact that you have the physique for the job."

Martha: "I bet he has a crush on you."

Lauren: "Cut it out, would you? This is embarrassing. Although, he's cute…"

Michèle: "Give me a break. He's a baby. I feel sorry for this generation, you know. Everybody is optimistic about the future, but I see a trend toward materialism in a pejorative sense, a preoccupation for money and success devoid of humanistic values. My daughter's life will be impoverished for that."

Kelly: "Unfortunately, I agree with you. All the signs are there. Foucault has been prophetic in *The Order of Things*, advancing the theory of the eventual collapse of human civilization, and even the effacement of the human being, as we move away from the order established in the human sciences."

Michèle: "*Man would be erased, like a face drawn in sand at the edge of the sea.* Very poetic, and very frightening."

Kelly: "Indeed. Technology is advancing by leaps and bounds. Ask our colleagues in computer science, they say that in twenty years we'll be living in the digital age, where most of our life functions will be taken over by computers. And each of us will have a personal computer."

Michèle: "Not only that, they say that computer microchips will then be implanted in the body, so that the body itself will become a computer. The danger looming ahead is that we may turn into machines."

Martha: "This was already a concern of the avant-garde artists at the turn of the century, with the appearance of the automobile, the airplane, the telephone and the other technological 'monsters.' It's up to us to ensure that this won't happen. We have a responsibility to instill strong humanistic principles in our students."

Lauren, with tongue in cheek: "Absolutely. And perhaps, someday they'll be able to build a robot with a human heart."

"Ha ha ha. This would be a good character for a comic book." I laughed and then turned serious. "Look, whatever will be, we cannot stop it. I leave it to the next generations to build their own world and be responsible for their own happiness... I want to say one thing, though. I'm glad I will no longer be around to share that 'brave new world' with them. I plan to make my exit as a human being."

Martha: "Let's drink to that!"

We raised our glasses of milkshake.

PART THREE

Today (2001-2011)

IV

New York, 2001

Here the manuscript ends. Or rather, it is interrupted. Toward the end of the eighties, Amy moved to New York to work with Larry at L&N. It was at that time that she lost track of Stella.

Stella's manuscript stayed with Amy for all these years, until she decided that it was time to bring it to life. This rough draft includes some of Amy's edits. She did not change the original manuscript substantially, but she had to intervene here and there to adjust the narrative, to make it more gripping, more interesting to the reader. In other words, she had to turn it into a novel because, let's face it, memoirs can be dull. However, she did not alter Stella's voice. After all, this is her story.

But the editing is not complete. Sitting at her desk, in the penthouse suspended in the dark sky, she realizes that there is still a lot of work to do. For example, to change the names of the main characters in order to protect their real identity. What would be a good name for Jim?... Scott? Harry? Amy is undecided. Also, she'll have to find another name for Villa Flora, and for Rosa, and Larry, and all the others. And then she'll have to write a conclusion. That will not be difficult, though. Amy has enough imagination to come up with a plausible closure. Or lack of it. An open ending, skillfully devised, may actually add more meaning to the story. It will underscore the inexorable march of history, the passing of an epoch, and the uncertainty of the future.

It will take Amy a couple of years to finish the job. Her workdays are full, and it is only at night that she can turn to the manuscript.

And what about the byline? Better use a pen name and leave the author unidentified. The mystery surrounding the author may even turn out to be a brilliant commercial gimmick.

V

The book is an immediate hit. Presentation and press conference at the Ritz are followed by a VIP reception for three-hundred guests. A huge pile of copies, already signed by the mystery author, sold out in half an hour. Hundreds of questions from the reporters of the Style pages: can you give us a hint, is it a man or a woman, does he/she live in the States or Italy or somewhere else, is he/she alive, is this a real story that reflects the author's background? Amy's only answer is that she's not at liberty to violate the author's wish for privacy. Publishers from the other major presses offer their insincere congratulations, while pondering why in the hell didn't I think of this expedient myself. Literary agents work their way through the crowd and come over to her to pitch the latest writer of genius they recently discovered.

Amy is exhausted. The stress accumulated during the months preceding the launch suddenly comes down heavily on her. She cannot stand the glitz of the Ritz one minute longer. She dials L&N's vice president. He picks up his cell, Amy can see him by the bar, entertaining two bejeweled socialites. "Hey, Tom, I'm going to disappear. You're in charge." "Okey dokey, I'll take over. Have a good one, whatever you're going to do." Amy steals away, leaving behind friends and admirers and even her evening escort.

At home she falls into a deep sleep, and wakes up late in the morning when the phone rings.

She doesn't want to pick up, she doesn't want to talk to anyone, she wants to go back to sleep. Go away.

But the phone keeps ringing.

What the hell... "Hello!"

"Ciao, Stella."

A thunderbolt. Now, she is totally awake.

"Jim?!!"

"Who else calls you Stella?"

"No one."

"And so, it's me. I'm the only one who knows the identity of the mysterious author."

"My goodness, I can't believe it. After all these years... How're you doing? Where are you? Why..."

"Whoa, hold it. Take a deep breath and join me for lunch. We have a lot to catch up with. I'll meet you in an hour at the Tree Top Café."

Now, she is looking at him across the table, on the terrace overlooking the park.

He didn't change. Still handsome like thirty years ago. Even more. Time treated him well by adding a silvery reflection to the hair and a few expression lines to his magnetic blue eyes. The hair is shorter and well-trimmed, but a rebellious shock falls down on the forehead, a match to his mischievous grin.

"You didn't change," he tells her. "Still beautiful like thirty years ago. Even more."

"D'you really remember how I looked back then?"

"I certainly do. You had loose, soft curls. You still do, but they were a bit longer and darker. This new light shade of gold is actually very becoming. It matches the specks in your eyes and gives you an overall radiant look."

"Life taught you how to talk to a woman."

"Not really. I still say what I think. You *are* beautiful."

"In this case, I'm glad to hear that. You must have been around a lot of beautiful women."

"Yes, quite a few."

"D'you have a wife? Kids?"

"I had three wives. Just got divorce number three a month ago. No kids. What about you?"

"No more husbands after Steve. No kids."

"Why did you decide not to remarry?"

"I did not *decide*. I simply didn't feel I had to."

"You must have made a lot of men unhappy."

"Yes, quite a few."

"Is there a happy man in your life now?"

"No. No one so lucky at the moment."

The host of a popular TV talk show walks by their table.

"Amy, dear, how can you look so wonderful after last night? I'm still recovering. What a great party. And a smashing success. You're booked for an interview next week, don't forget."

"If it's on my calendar, I'll be there. It'll be a pleasure, really." The TV guy looks at Jim and greets him with a nod. "Ah, Jason, you know James Welsh, don't you?"

"Mr. Welsh, glad to see you. It's been a while since you were on my show. How about another appearance? Perhaps just before the release of your next movie."

"You should talk to my agent, she handles my schedule. But, in principle, I'll be glad to meet your audience again."

A few more pleasantries and the guy is gone.

"How does it feel to be a celebrity?" Jim asks.

"I should ask you the same question. I saw all your movies of the past ten years, the really good ones, you know, after you moved to New York and became an independent producer. You created your own brand, and I love it."

"It feels good to have a fan like you. I used to rely on your judgement in the old days."

"And I on yours. You've not commented on my novel yet."

"I was about to do that. Over the years I read your books on literary theory and criticism, and I knew you were an insightful thinker and a good writer. But it's hard to believe that this is your first novel. It's literature at its best, and at the same time it's an engaging story that pleases the reader, with intriguing characters and a dynamic plot. A very accomplished work."

"Well, I had good material to work with…" She flashes him a knowing glance.

"Undoubtedly." A spark of complicit laughter flickers in his eyes.

We're still a team, Amy thinks.

"Where's 'Stella' these days?"

"Nowhere to be seen, or better, heard. One day I realized that my childhood friend was no longer needed. I used to discuss issues with her, back and forth, every time I was to make a decision. It really helped me. She was the cautionary voice in the debate. She tried to pull me back and make me think before jumping into action, although my instinct often prevailed. Then, our voices merged. And I let go of her."

"When you first told me about Stella, I thought you chose a wonderful name for your fantasy friend, a guiding star. Calling you that, I felt some magic dust might sprinkle down on me as well."

"Obviously, it worked. You've come a long way."

They go out that night. And then, the next. And then, every night.

That first night, Jim takes her home and dismisses the driver.

The doorman opens the door. Jim puts an arm around her shoulders to escort her inside. She stops and turns to him.

"Good night, love. Let's give ourselves some time."

He looks puzzled.

"Thirty years is not enough?"

She is not in a hurry to invite him into her bed. She needs a friend, not a lover, although... She is in his arms now, his embrace is strong, their lips almost touch... She wants him, like she did back then. But a friend is such a precious thing. She never had another one after Jim, a real friend with whom to share every thought and every feeling. Sex tends to complicate things. She had too many sex relations. She needs a friend.

"Let's talk about it tomorrow. Would you like to kiss me good night?" She says it lightly to break the spell of the moment.

"I would like to kiss you *all* night," he answers seriously.

His kiss is sweet, enticing.

She gently breaks away.

"I'm so happy you're again in my life," she tells him.

And she walks through the door, alone.

They go out the next night. And then, every night.

For a whole week, Jim shows up at her office sharply at 5:00. If she is still in a meeting, he hangs out with the staff. Many editors are now women, smart and elegant and even too eager to entertain him. He flirts with each of them and charms them all. Those who remember the old days at the press say that it feels like Larry is back.

They spend a couple of hours every day discussing a joint project before going out for a night on the town. They avoid all official events—both their personal assistants keep busy responding to dozens of invitations with regrets notes. They go to the Village for some jazz, catch a play off-Broadway, stop for dinner in an unknown *trattoria* that happens to be on their way when they get tired of walking, visit the studio of an artist friend in Soho.

They are young again. She feels a surge of energy, the air vibrates more intensely, the hours are shortened by expectation, the instant is extended by total immersion. They fit together perfectly, like the two halves of the moon when they are joined to show the disc in its fullness. Words flow from where the discourse was interrupted, cleaned of the misunderstandings that drove them apart. A thirty-year gap is erased.

Every night, Jim takes her home. They kiss before the stone-faced doorman. And she walks through the door, alone.

Then, in bed, she thinks of him. She wants him by her side. She wants to feel the warmth of his body, she wants to be 'kissed all night.' She left him standing all alone on the sidewalk. A lonely figure in the urban desert. Desolation. Tomorrow she'll ask him in.

But she doesn't. Tomorrow is like today and the day before.

They are in her office, the papers spread out on the conference table, bottled water replaces the coffee mugs of old. Everybody has left, except for a few who are working against deadlines in the privacy of their rooms. The place is quiet.

Tom pokes his head in.

"Hey, guys, it's late. I'm leaving. Should I order you a pizza or something on my way out?"

"No, thanks. We're almost done," Amy tells him.

"Well, have fun."

He's gone.

"The more we talk about it, the more I like it," Jim says going back to their project. He came up with the idea of an adaptation of *Stella's Story* for the big screen. They spent the whole week putting together a deal and drafting the pre-production plan.

"It's not just a human interest story," he continues, "it's a story of social and historical significance. It unfolds over forty years of American history. We'll have to highlight that background with mass scenes, dynamic action, perhaps some documentary footage, because those facts help us understand how we got to where we're now."

"We're not in a good place, are we?"

"No. We have a president who's not really been elected by the people, but selected by the Supreme Court. That was a political act that discredited one of our most sacred institutions. It put us on a slippery slope because when the institutions are discredited the nation collapses."

"I often think of the good old Clinton days. Peace and prosperity, remember? That was only four years ago. When he left there was a budget surplus, which now has melted like ice-cream in the sun."

"Yes. Those were good years. But that prick really blew it in the end. The Clinton sex scandal, in a way, contributed to the blunder of the Bush 'selection.'"

"And now, this war in Iraq. What were they thinking? I mean Bush himself, but also his advisors and the Congress. Only someone totally ignorant of history could have made such an irresponsible decision."

Jim got up and poured himself a glass of water. No more coffee. No more cigarettes.

"Idiots! They dragged the nation into a misguided war instead of destroying those ragheads in Afghanistan who attacked us. We're paying for it with money and blood, and the result will be a destabilized Middle East with an empowered Iran, and with insurgent Islamic factions whose ultimate goal is to spread terrorism around the world and achieve total hegemony."

"And yet, there's no student revolt against this war like there was against the Vietnam War. The young seem to be rather indifferent."

"It's because there is no draft this time around. They don't have to fear for their skin. War exists in another dimension, in a land they don't even know how to find over the map. They confuse CNN images of combat with video games."

"Not all are like that."

"No, not all. Many volunteer for economic reasons, it's a job, and there aren't many jobs available nowadays. Some, for a spirit of adventure, an exotic land, killing the enemy, excitment. A few, for patriotism. They still believe in serving the country with honor and valor."

"At least, they receive better treatment when they come home than did the vets of the Vietnam War. It's almost like the nation wants to make amend for a past wrong."

"It seems so. In reality, we only pay lip service to them. They receive a heroes' welcome, but often remain homeless and unemployed."

"Is there anything we can do?"

"Ultimately, the health of a nation depends on its people. When the people become complacent, indifferent, disinterested in the politics at the top, and do not hold their leaders accountable, one ends up with a failed state. I'm not advocating 'the revolution!' 'People power!' 'Kill the pigs!'… No, you know me. I'm talking about responsible civil involvement. Education is essential. Our film may help, if we find the right angle."

"I hope so… Well, let's call it quits for today. I'm dying for a glass of champagne."

In one of the offices down the hall someone has put on an old disk, *I came back to let you know/Got a thing for you/And I can't let go.* The volume is low. They barely hear the music as they walk out.

In the elevator, Jim is pensive and inwardly focused. It seems he is still pondering over the conversation they had. But, actually, he has something else on his mind. Something that has to do with the two of them. To lighten him up, Amy teases him.

"You've created a lot of excitement among the staff. I mean, the women. They used to rush out for happy hours at the end of the day, and now they're not in a hurry to leave when you show up. Who wins your heart so far?"

"You won it long ago." His voice is firm. His gaze, steadfast.

He takes her in his arms. They kiss. A fifty-floor-long kiss. A burning kiss, she catches fire. The elevator stops in the lobby. He does not release her from his embrace.

"Tonight we're going to change direction," he says decidedly. And pushes the UP button to the penthouse.

The next day is warm and sunny, a gorgeous late September day. They are lying on a chaise by the pool. The chaise is large enough for the two of them, but small enough to keep them snug. On the table nearby are the remains of their breakfast.

Jim leans up on his elbow, and his eyes caress Amy's body from top to toe. His other hand rests on her thigh.

"You're still a great fuck."

"You're still the same old rascal. I thought you had become more sensitive at your mature age."

He laughs. "It was supposed to be a compliment. A very sincere one... I'm crazy about you."

"You're crazy, period."

"But you love me anyway." He gives her his irresistible roguish smile.

No response.

"Come here, let's make peace."

They make peace, and they make love.

They spend the whole weekend at home. The maid got two days off, and the phones are disconnected. They move from the bedroom to the pool to the bedroom to the kitchen... Neither of them feels like cooking. After they run out of supplies, mainly smoked salmon and brie, they go for a bite to eat at the fast-food joint down on the corner. No hamburger has ever tasted so good. Amy is famished. And she is happy. They are happy together. They smile at each other across the funky plastic table, while sinking their teeth into that yellow-mustarded delight.

They are happy together. But they do not talk about moving in together. They have their home, their habits, their weird schedules. They see each other regularly when they are both in New York. But their professional engagements often involve traveling, and keep them apart.

Other priorities prevent them from advancing the film project at a sustained pace. After one year, they decide to put it on the back burner until they can devote to it their uninterrupted attention.

Around that time Amy's trips to Italy become more frequent. Mother is still in good health, but with age she has become extremely fragile. Amy feels the urge to be with her. At first, she stays for a week or ten days. Then, as time goes by, she extends her visits up to an entire month. Tom replaces her at the office, and she runs the press long distance thanks to the magic of online connection—how was business even possible before email?

In her childhood home, Amy occupies the bedroom that has always been hers. Nothing in there has changed. Even her teenage mini-skirts are still hanging in the closet, and the calendar on the desk has not been advanced beyond the year 1967.

Mother walks in before retiring for the night and sits down on the soft chair by the bed. Amy puts down the book she is reading, and they start talking. Hours go by. This is their quiet time together, after the domestic hustle and bustle of the day. "There's no peace in this house. I only wish they'd leave me alone," is mother's constant refrain. *They* are the maid, the caregiver, the therapist, the next-door neighbor paying a visit, the decorator replacing the drapes, a cousin showing off her grandchildren… and other similar pains in the neck. Anna has always been a private person, cherishing her secluded world like all artists do. But after breaking her hip, she became outright intolerant of others. Having to depend on someone else's care is hard to take. She seeks only Amy's company.

She is still very beautiful. Wavy snow-white hair at ear length, parted in the middle, a pale and smooth complexion, rare at her age, eyes like sparkling amber. When Amy was little, she looked at her in awe and thought to herself, "When I grow up I'll be like her." It never happened. Although, people say that she took after her mother.

Anna sits in the soft chair by the bed, like she did when Amy was a kid. But she is not there to read her a fairy tale.

"Have you noticed that today I walked around the house without the cane? The therapist said that perhaps next week I can go out for a stroll."

"That's marvelous. We can go to the Grand Café for tea, like we used to. Hope they still have those delicious chocolate truffles."

"Let's do that. And then, we may go to Villa Flora for a few days. I've not been there at all this summer."

"We'll do that as well."

"And then… But when are you leaving?"

"Don't worry about that. I can stay a little longer. And when I leave, it'll be only for a short while. I'll be back soon."

"You know, I'm glad you have a life over there. That's where you ought to be. When I named you America, I did not have any precise reason for that. I liked the fact that it was an unusual name for a girl, and also a reference to your father. But when you decided to leave and make it on your own, I realized that the name was well chosen, it fit your personality. You needed vast horizons and clear skies, where you could unleash your potential. Italy was too small a place for you, stifling, with no opportunities for young people."

"But what about you? Why did you choose to stay?"

"I'm an artist. An artist is free no matter where she is. Besides, I have always lived in the margins, spending most of the time at Villa Flora and traveling a lot. I, too, ran away from the stultifying living rooms of the well-to-do."

"You know, often I felt nostalgic and sort of guilty for leaving you. At the same time, I felt that you wanted me to go after my dreams and aspirations, and with time I realized that while living our separate lives we never got really apart, the bond between us remained strong."

"True. Over all these years I have always felt your presence in this house. As if you were just in the other room and I could easily reach out to you. It was a happy feeling, like an anticipation of our next reunion. But now I think, what if I'm no longer here when she comes back?"

"You should not think that way."

"I often think about death."

"You should think about life. You had a wonderful life. You were free to live the way you wanted, free to devote yourself to art… Is there something you would have done differently?"

"I have no regrets. I played my cards and enjoyed the challenge. It was exciting. But in the game of life, sadly to say, there are no winners."

"I don't understand."

"Of course you don't. Not now. But you will."

Her smile is serene and sad. She is remote, in a place beyond Amy's reach. Amy takes her hand.

"Are you happy?"

"Happy? I don't think this word applies to my condition. Happy is a young people's attribute. I'm not unhappy, though. But that's different."

"Have you been happy with dad?"

"Very happy. We've been in love."

"But you refused to marry him."

"These two things do not necessarily go together. You must be true to yourself first of all. Marriage was not for me. And certainly, not for him either. At first he had a hard time understanding my position. He felt rejected. But then, we spent many happy days together, at Villa Flora, in New York, traveling around the world for my shows… He's been the ideal companion. I never thought of him as a husband."

"I loved him too."

"And now, whom do you love? Is Jim still around?"

"Why d'you ask? I've been with him for a couple of years now. You know that."

"Next time, you should take him along. I was fond of him when he came to visit at Villa Flora in the old days. He's brilliant and charming, perhaps brash at times, but deep down he has a vulnerable spot. Don't hurt him again."

What d'you mean? Amy wants to ask. She needs to hear more. About Jim, about Larry, about love, how to love, about life, how to live, how to die… Mother, tell me.

But Anna gets up and slowly walks toward the door.

"I need to get some rest. There's no peace in this house. Sleep well, darling." The door closes softly behind her.

She cannot tell her. Perhaps she has the answers, but only for herself. Amy has to find her own.

VI

New York, 2011

Pizzeria Santa Lucia. Expanded and redecorated (again!) in the finest contemporary design, it is now the hub of the intellectuals chic who look for organic tomatoes, imported buffalo mozzarella, and geographically identified wines bottled at the vineyard—for 'slow food', in short. Here, one can be sure to run into authors and artists, famous and would-be-famous, and topnotch journalists.

At a table a party of six is celebrating—Rosa, Joe, Chris, his wife Peggy, Amy and Dan, her current companion. It is a family celebration, and Amy feels lucky to be considered as part of the family. She also feels awkward for having brought Dan along. It's obvious that he does not belong.

Joe raises his glass.

"We're so blessed. We've got so many things to celebrate that I don't even know where to start, and when we're finished celebrating we'll all be drunk. So, first thing first. Let's drink to this happy couple, us, Rosa and me. Today we celebrate our 45th anniversary. Thank you, honey, it's been a wonderful journey." They kiss. They are obviously still in love. "I remember when we first met, in Villa Flora's beautiful gardens... you were a flower yourself. I picked you and transplanted you into the hard ground of this city, and you kept blooming, resilient, through the good and the bad times."

"Cheers!!"

"And this brings me to the second reason for celebration. Five years ago, Amy, your mom put Villa Flora up for sale. It was deteriorating, no more flowers in the gardens, and the winery was on the brink of going bankrupt. We were going to lose our best wine supplier. I decided to buy the property. It turned out to be a good deal for us, although it took us five years to turn it into a profitable business. Chris restored the villa to its original splendor and turned it into a five-star hotel, and I was able to revive the vineyards and bring the winery back to full production. Just last week we had the first order shipped to a large wine distributor here in the States. So, first we drank to love, now let's drink to business."

"Well, it's business and love together because you bought Villa Flora as a gift to Rosa. At least, this is what you told us," Peggy says.

"This makes for a good reverse of fortune story." Dan's ironical comment sounds inappropriate and rude. He's definitely not attuned to the spirit of the company.

Rosa looks embarrassed. She takes Amy's hand, "Amy, how d'you feel about this whole thing? I never really asked but, after all, it was your grandma's house. Now everything changed, it's sort of upside down… Are you sure you're comfortable with that?"

"I'm absolutely comfortable, don't worry. It's been a win-win for everyone. Mom got a good price for the property and was happy to see it restored and well managed. And I can go and stay at the hotel whenever I feel nostalgic."

Chris: "Well, talking about success, I must brag a little. The restoration of Villa Flora brought us a lot of new business. Many of our American clients now want us to find and restore properties for them in Italy. Last year we had to open a studio in Milan."

Pop!… Another bottle of prosecco. "Cheers!!"

Joe: "Chris is doing great. We're very proud of you, son.

You know, my father was devoted to St. Christopher and that's why we named you after him. Perhaps, you enjoy some special protection from up there. In any case, let's not forget that what we have today is the result of my parents' legacy. Rocco and Lucia built the base for us to succeed with their hard work, optimism, and love of country. I'm proud of being the son of immigrants and a true American."

"Cheers!!"

Dan: "I wish we could say the same about the millions of Latino immigrants who today are unwelcomed and facing deportation."

Oh, no. Dan is going into political mode. Amy hates it when he does. He's blinded by political correctness.

Joe: "You're talking about illegal immigrants, I guess."

Dan: "You call them illegal because they are undocumented, but they are just immigrants who come here to seek a better life."

Chris: "Wait a minute. There's no equivalence between my grandparents who asked for permission to enter the U.S., were legally admitted, pledged allegiance to this country and did their best to learn the language and to integrate, and these people who break the law, violate our border, and want to impose their language and culture on us. If they love America, they should come in the legal way. But if all they want is to take advantage of us, they should stay out."

Dan: "We have a humanitarian crisis on our hands. Children are being separated from their parents. We should open up our hearts."

Joe: "This is a crisis of their own making. Families should stay together and apply for a visa. Look, this is still the land of opportunities—not for long, if things keep going the way they do under this administration. But, what I want to say is that we as a country do appreciate the immigrants' contribution. Chris in construction, I at the restaurant, between the two of us we employ dozens of Latinos. It's not a matter of discrimination. However, you must be honest with yourself and not allow anyone to play you for a fool."

Dan: "What d'you mean?"

Joe: "Well, the issue is being distorted by the liberal left and in the media…"

Chris: "Excuse me, Dad. Let me answer this. To put it plainly, you liberals play the humanitarian card to advance your own agenda. You don't care for those poor devils, you just want to enlarge your constituency, give the vote to illegals, and grab the power permanently."

Dan: "I… I don't…"

Chris: "I'm not finished. You are hypocrites. You don't care that unregulated immigration places a financial burden on our schools, our hospitals, our welfare system, at a time when our own people are struggling for lack of jobs. You think only of your political games while wrapping yourselves up in the mantle of social justice. And instead of justice all you achieve is poverty and more poverty for everyone."

Dan: "But…"

Chris: "And there's more. There's also an aspect of national security involved. Together with the workers, criminal elements infiltrate our country. And not just common criminals involved with drugs and human trafficking, but most likely terrorists from other parts of the world who may use our southern border as a point of entry."

The situation is deteriorating. Rosa is worried. She pats Chris on the arm—Easy, son—But Chris gets all worked up. So does Dan.

Dan: "Those who are obsessed with border security are xenophobic morons who see an enemy in every foreigner."

Chris: "Go ahead, keep mouthing your party trooper talking points and you'll wake up screaming one of these days, like we all did on 9/11. We were here. We saw the people injured, shocked, come in and take refuge in this very room. That was only the beginning. Now we're almost done rebuilding a magnificent tower, a monument to the indomitable American spirit. But we're still under attack by those same guys, and the next strike will be even worse."

Dan: "We deserve what we get for our involvement in the Middle East. If only we helped those guys to get good jobs and treated them with respect, they wouldn't be angry at us."

Chris: "Yeah, and they would return the favor by chopping our heads off more gently, with anesthesia perhaps. You're a disgrace. You brainwashed skunk. Get out of here."

Dan gets up and reaches out for Amy's hand. She doesn't move. He hesitates, wants to say something. Then changes his mind, turns around, and leaves.

A moment of silence. Nobody at the other tables seems to have noticed the incident. The waiters move swiftly over the floor. The wine pours in many shades of red. Soft conversation, laughter, happy faces.

Chris collects himself, drives his fingers through the hair, as if to smooth down his thoughts. "I'm sorry," he says, "I got carried away. Very sorry I ruined the evening for everyone. Especially for you, Amy."

"It's my fault, I shouldn't have brought Dan along. We've been together for a while and I'm fond of him. He's a professor of history at Columbia, where I teach a course in creative writing. He has a lot of interesting things to say… as long as it does not get to politics, then he becomes stiffly doctrinaire."

"It's impossible to have a serious discussion with people like him," says Joe.

"He's a nice guy. But he's one of many among the faculty who in their youth fell under the spell of Saul Alinsky, you know, the first community organizer. They were in love with his teachings and still pledge allegiance to him."

"With Obama as president those teachings came back into fashion," Chris commented. "These guys didn't notice that the country has changed since the sixties. There have been reforms, anti-discrimination laws, social progress. This is no longer the time for revolutionary tactics. It is the time to get together and collaborate for the common good. We don't need leaders who divide us in order to gain more control. We need leaders willing to unify the nation. Either we change the president with this mid-term election, or our country will sadly turn into a Banana Republic."

Diego comes over, "Everything okay, boss?" He looks around the table, "Can I get you anything else? More wine?"

Everybody says, "No, we're fine."

"An espresso for me, please," says Joe.

Diego darts away.

"He's such a bright guy," Rosa says fondly. "He's from Honduras, all papers in order. In less than six months he's become our head waiter."

Joe: "It's odd, but Italian restaurants can't find Italian personnel anymore, unless it's a renowned chef. Those who come to the U.S. from Italy nowadays are young people with college degrees, who get high-paying jobs or become successful entrepreneurs in all fields—finance, science, architecture, you name it."

Chris: "This trend started some time ago, already in the seventies. Amy is an example of it."

"True. But for me it was a bit easier because of my dad."

Joe: "No, no, you should take all the credit. You went through grad school and had an academic career. And then, you've done a heck of a job running the press after Larry departed. It's not easy these days with everything going digital, ebooks saturating the market, and all those new gadgets. And yet, you keep putting out one bestseller after another. And I mean, real paper books."

Rosa: "My favorite is *Stella's Story*. When did it come out? Five, six years ago? It's been a while, but I still think about it. In a way, it is also a story of immigration. It talked to me."

Chris: "It also talked to millions of other readers, judging by the number of copies sold. But its success has also to do with the mystery involving the author. We're still speculating about the author's identity, and so are the critics, and the readers even set up betting games on Facebook."

The last few customers unhurriedly get up and walk toward the exit. Diego lets them out before locking the door.

The waiters are busy cleaning the tables and resetting them for the next day.

Chris and Peggy take leave.

Joe goes out to the patio for his daily smoke—one cigarette a day is all Rosa allows.

"I better get going. I lost my driver and I have to call a cab." Amy is fumbling with her iPhone.

Rosa stops her. "Wait! It's unfortunate what happened with Dan. Are you okay?"

"I'm fine. It had to happen, one way or the other. The relation was getting stale. This incident ended it naturally, and spared me a Dear John note."

"You're amazing. You have an ability to turn everything into positives. I was stunned two years ago, when Jim remarried for the fourth time, and things between the two of you instead of breaking up even improved. Now, you two are the best of friends...—Oh, what's that?"

Someone is knocking on the front door. Diego parts the curtains slightly.

"It's your granddaughter," he says, and lets her in.

"Ellen! You're a bit late for the celebration, darling."

"Hi, Granny." Kiss kiss. "I came to pick up mom and dad. Knowing how generously wine flows on your table, I did not want them to drive."

"Well, they're gone. Don't worry, they'll be alright. Perhaps you may give Amy a lift. You do remember Amy, don't you?"

"I certainly remember *you*," Amy says, "although you've changed a lot since last time I saw you."

"She's now a freshman in college," Rosa fills her in.

"I'll turn eighteen in two weeks," Ellen says proudly. "You should come to my party."

"Are you sure I'm not too old for that crowd?"

"Absolutely sure. There's going to be people all ages, in the best Italian style. Right, Granny?" And, as an aside, "She's picking up the tab."

"Right. A large extended family. Really, Amy, do come. And bring Jim along. Ellen's friends will be thrilled to meet someone from the movies."

"In that case, I can't refuse."

VII

Two weeks later

The party is going to take place at Chris's beach house in the Hamptons. Amy and Jim have resumed the film project, and he is glad of this occasion to meet with young people and get their perspective on where we are standing at this juncture as a nation.

As they drive along the shoreline, the house appears on a rise behind the dunes. The sun is still high and accentuates its whiteness. The house shines, suspended between sky and ocean.

"Wow! It's a mansion. It could be a movie set for a Fitzgerald story," Jim marvels.

"And yet, it's brand new. You know, Chris is an architect. This is his dream house."

The cell rings. Jim activates the speaker phone.

"Yes, honey, what's up?"

"Honey my foot. You took the Porsche without telling me, and now I have to drive the Volvo, which I detest."

"Why don't you take the Mercedes? That is *your* car."

"I smashed it last week. Don't you remember? It's still at the body shop. But, of course, you don't pay any attention to what happens to me."

"Colleen, I'm just arriving now. Can we postpone this conversation?"

"Go to hell!" Click.

Jim smiles at Amy, embarrassed. "Sorry for involving you in domestic squabbles."

"She sounded quite upset."

"She is constantly upset. The car was just a pretext."

"Perhaps she's right that you don't pay enough attention to her."

"Perhaps she is. But I can't help it." He shrugs. He is visibly annoyed. Amy does not probe any deeper.

Jim turns onto the driveway and passes by the tennis court, the pool, and a large lawn, where a white tent has been set up for the party.

The guests are strolling, drink in hand, greeting each other, forming small groups. The kids run all over the lawn without direction, screaming for no other reason than the joy of being alive. The band sets up the instruments for the dance. Two long tables are soon to be covered with an array of gourmet dishes—no pizza! Ellen ordered.

She is the center of attention, beautiful in a light pink dress that enhances her tanned body and long black curls.

She sees them and moves in their direction.

"Hi, I'm so glad you came. And this is really James Welsh. *The* James Welsh?" She looks at Jim with dreaming eyes.

"Hi, Ellen. Thank you for having me at your party," Jim says.

"Where's Rosa?" Amy asks, looking around.

"Granny is applying the finishing touches to the buffet. She'll be out soon. The rest of the family is mingling with the guests. But I wanted to grab you two. Get a drink and join my friends. They are dying to meet you."

Ellen's friends hang out on the deck overlooking the ocean, among wicker furniture, potted plants and large umbrellas stylishly arranged.

"This is Andy, my brother. Amy, you already know him. And those are... Guys, you'll introduce yourselves. There's too many of you."

Amy and Jim are surrounded by gorgeous specimens of the gilded youth. "Hi, I'm Charles." "Tony." "Susie." "Louise." "Alan." "Roy." "Maya."... others.

Amy looks for words to start a conversation in a challenging way, skipping the usual platitudes.

Jim beats her. "Hi, guys. I missed you."

"You missed... *us*?" asks Andy.

"Yes. I used to teach at a college in California in the late sixties. Amy was there, too. After that, I met with people your age only on rare occasions."

"What did you teach?" Charles wants to know.

"Film studies."

"Fabulous! Film studies, in California, in the sixties. For us that is such a romantic time," Susie says.

Roy jumps in. "My grandfather told us kids a lot of stories about the sixties. Although, he's is from Alabama. A different set up altogether. He was a young black fighting for civil rights."

"Did he meet Dr. King?" Tony asks.

"You bet, he did. He went marching in Selma."

"Wow! That makes him a historical figure."

"I guess so. He should be honored for that. Instead, nowadays he's not even welcome to speak on campuses."

"Where on campuses?"

"Mostly the elitist ones, you know, those that are considered 'progressive', the Ivy-League type. Look, my grandfather was a top-grade student, got a scholarship and went to medical school, and became a renowned heart surgeon. And now, because he's pro-life and defends the true spirit of the civil rights movement, the liberals want to silence him."

"I'm pro-choice, but I'm for open discussion," says Louise. "Those who don't share our views have a right to speak out. Unfortunately, it's getting pretty ugly. On our campus the liberals have unleashed the thought police among the students. You can only exercise your freedom of speech in designated areas, heavily patrolled. And they call themselves Democrats. I guess your grandfather is a Democrat as well."

"Not anymore. You kidding? If you've got half a brain, you cannot be a Democrat today. The Democratic Party of old no longer exists. It's been hijacked by a bunch of ideologues with a loud voice that prevails over all others."

"I take you won't vote for Obama's second term." Jim's quip adds fuel to the fire.

"No way! In '08 it was my first election and I was excited. Obama was someone new and fresh on the political scene, he fired us up with the promise of 'change', and so I voted for him..."

"And also because he's black," Maya interjects. She sits next to Roy and has an arm around his shoulders. They are obviously a couple.

"I can understand black pride. But then, why did so many white people vote for him?" Jim looks around to draw the others into the conversation.

"I didn't vote. I was only fifteen." This is Ellen.

Roy again: "Being black really helped him. A white man without a track record, lacking executive experience and political qualifications, would never have made it. White Americans, whether you like it or not, are still saddled with a guilt complex about slavery. There are those who flaunt their racial sensitivities by sustaining any black cause, no matter what. And the Democrats play the race card to their political advantage. That's why he got so many white votes."

"This time around it'll be different," Louise intervenes. "We don't like the kind of 'change' he wants to implement. We're told not to love our country and not to be proud of it, but to work for its fundamental transformation. That's what we hear from our political leaders, the president himself, our professors in most universities, and the mainstream media."

"Guys, you forget that the transformation has already occurred on many levels over the past forty years, thanks to the movements of the 60s. They produced positive results. Minorities, women, and gays acquired rights that made our society more equal and just. But more needs to be done. The transformation must be radical. We must go all the way and adopt a socialist system," says Alan.

"Alan's the only radical voice here," Ellen tells Jim under her breath. "He's a philosophy student, and normally he wears a T-shirt that says, 'I ♥ Marx'. It's coming back into fashion. He's sort of out of place in this group of business and science majors, but we love him anyway."

"Especially you," says Susie, nudging her. They giggle and exchange a conniving look.

Alan is about to embark in a long tirade, but Ellen takes him by the hand. "Let's go dancing," she says sweetly. They walk out.

Jim is totally engrossed in the discussion, following the arguments that dart back and forth.

Amy steals away, hoping to find Rosa among the guests. The band is now playing. Several couples are on the dance floor. Crossing the lawn, Amy catches fragments of conversation. It seems that politics are on everybody's mind.

"...then, something went wrong. I am concerned with the recent trend. Have you noticed that our fundamental values as a nation have eroded? Especially among the young." An attractive soccer-mom is talking to a distinguished older gentleman.

"Absolutely, and who's to blame? Obama goes around the world apologizing for U.S. past policies, primarily to the Arab countries. He exposes the United States to public humiliation. Look, I do not justify Bush's wars in any way. He made a series of big mistakes that put us on the wrong path. But we should acknowledge our mistakes, correct them the best we can, and still be proud of our country. Instead, by his words and actions, Obama seems to dislike the U.S. and the Western values in general, while leaning toward the Muslim world."

A younger guy, probably her husband, joins the conversation. "No surprise. His middle name is Hussein, and he's been educated in the *madrasas* of Indonesia. He himself describes that period in his autobiography as a formative experience."

Amy spots Rosa with a tray of drinks moving toward a table where Joe sits with a group of friends of Italian descent. They tend to stick together, feeling a special bond to each other.

"Rosa, sit down. Let the waiters do the job. Relax!" Joe prompts her. Then, he sees Amy approaching. "Amy, come and join us. Where were you hiding?"

Everybody greets the women, and the conversation around the table picks up from where it was left.

"As I was saying," —a portly, mustachioed man resumes his train of thought, — "our president knows how to play the victim card well. And his party *apparatchiki* trumpet his message and indoctrinate the most vulnerable. They are masters at that. They are succeeding in dividing the country, pitting the people against each other—rich and poor, black and white, men and women, citizens and police... So much for the promises of the Unifier-in-Chief. By dividing the people, they are spreading the victim syndrome virus."

A matron, her ears and neck dressed up with tons of gold jewelry, jumps in. "True. We used to be a country of achievers, until not long ago. Our elders arrived without a penny. If someone was rich and successful they strove to emulate him, and we followed in their steps. We looked up to the successful people. Not anymore. Now, the message we get is not emulation, but envy: he's rich and successful, that's not fair, so you should demand a share of his wealth. Pride is lost. And this culture of envy in turn leads to the culture of entitlement. That's not good for our children."

"Connie, you hit the nail on the head." Her husband pats her manicured, plump hand. "The victim syndrome is taking roots in all sectors of society, everybody feels oppressed, everybody needs help. It's a political gimmick to emasculate the people and make them dependent on the government. The nanny state promises free stuff, and takes away pride and dignity. Food stamps, free housing, free cell phones…"

Rosa cannot stay put for long. She has to move around, supervise, give directions, help out… She excuses herself. Amy follows her, but, realizing Rosa is too busy for a chat, she gives up and goes back to the deck.

There the young people are still passionately involved in sorting out the current situation.

Jim fetches from the buffet a large plate of grilled shrimp and lobster for everybody, and a mug of beer for himself. He puts the plate on the coffee table and resumes his place in the group.

Roy reaches out for a shrimp, while finishing his point.

"…You don't solve the problem of poverty and urban violence with welfare. Certainly not within the black community. You only aggravate it."

This seems to tie in with the conversation Amy has just left behind. Is anyone interested in any other topic? Apparently not. She finds a quiet spot for herself, from where she can observe the action without participating.

Alan comes back with Ellen from the dance floor, ruddy cheeks and glowing eyes. "Aggravate it? A social safety net is absolutely necessary in a rich country like ours. The government must protect the poor from the sharks of Wall Street."

Roy: "No doubt. But look, the blacks obtained their rights in the sixties fighting for themselves. Then they entered the middle class through their initiative and labor, with just a little help from Uncle Sam—Affirmative Action was necessary at that time, as was the GI Bill for thousands of vets. But later the system got corrupted. The party leaders figured out that they could use the minorities in order to get more votes. And so, the larger the number of social programs, the larger their constituency. Now the system is broken. Today forty percent of the population is on some form of welfare. And the number is growing."

Charles, balancing two tall drinks in both hands, sits down cautiously next to Louise on a cushioned couch. "And the other sixty percent pay for it. The leftists call it 'redistribution of wealth,' and Obama is its great advocate. Remember the '08 campaign, when he was addressed by a plumber in the crowd on this subject? He openly admitted he was for it. So, his current policies are actually consistent with his political agenda."

Louise, sipping from her glass: "But this is un-American. Who authorized them to take from me and give to others? I understand the Christian exhortation to take care of your neighbor. That's an individual impulse, an act of love spontaneous and free, a person-to-person relation. What those guys up there do is totally different. It's an imposition, an institutionalized mandate to give to *them*, the government, so that they can use, and misuse, the money according to their plans and interests. There's no compassion in this equation, only calculated politics."

Alan: "The end justifies the means. Alms thrown at the beggars on church steps will not solve anything. It is only through a calculated, scientific system that we're going to achieve social justice."

Jim has not interfered so far. But now he can't keep quiet.

"You mean a socialist system on the model of the Soviet Union? That one went up in flames. It imploded from within. And even the socialist democracies of Europe are now in big trouble." How to make someone like Alan understand this simple fact? If only he would use his brain instead of memorizing propaganda booklets lines, he would see that a fair system is one that affords every citizen equal opportunity, not equal income. That the pie will never be divided into equal parts. That this is a myth, a political con job for the gullible. He would see that the larger the pie, the more everyone benefits from it, proportionally. That the key to prosperity is economic growth. This has been one of our guiding principles until now. And the proof that it works is that nowhere in the history of mankind has such a large majority of the population, the middle class, reached such a high standard of living as in our society.

Susie's cheerful voice jolts him out of his reflections. "Go Millennials! Let's save our country!" She gets up and starts a cheerleader routine, flinging her legs up in the air under Tony's appreciative gaze.

Charles: "Good idea. Tomorrow I'll go get myself a bumper sticker. Jokes aside, if we are serious about doing something we should start with saving our language."

"You mean declaring English the national language and cancelling classes in Spanish for Latino children?" Alan's tone is half ironic, half challenging.

Charles: "No. I'm referring to something much deeper and more insidious. I'm talking about the scourge of political correctness. The PC police squads are turning the kids into a generation of idiots."

Susie: "True. I really miss Christmas at school. You know, the decorations, the lights, the parties. And also at my little sister's school. It happens at all levels. They say Christmas is not PC."

Tony: "They argue that it's about the separation of Church and State. But then they want to ban the Christmas tree, which is a pagan symbol. Perhaps, we should call it 'Little Spruce' like they do in Russia. With that name it was allowed even in Soviet times."

Charles: "It's all a matter of language. It is a malicious control game."

Andy jumps down from the railing where he was perched, and moves closer to those sitting in the circle. "Have you heard the latest? The designation M and W on toilet doors is not PC because it discriminates against transgenders."

Tony, managing to stand as close as possible next to Susie:

"Yes. In one school in California they allow students to use both the boys and the girls toilets, according to which gender they feel they are on a given day. For example, on Monday I'm a boy and use the boys' toilet. On Tuesday I'm a girl and use the girls' toilet. In other words, I'm the gender I *say* I am. And..."—he points a finger at Susie—"if you girls don't let me pee with you, you're very, very politically incorrect and must be suspended."

Susie punches him in the shoulder, and he reaches out to grab her. She laughs and runs, he runs after her.

Andy: "That's hard to top. But let me try. A friend of mine tells me that at the local school where he lives they have abolished the pronouns 'he' and 'she' because they are considered sexist, and have replaced them with the neutral 'ze'. So, when in a dispute you don't know who's right or wrong, you'll have to describe it as a 'ze said-ze said' situation."

Roy: "Oh, man. This can't be true."

Ellen: "It's hard to believe. But then, in the same spirit, at Target they've eliminated the Boys/Girls department signs. Now it's all a big mess."

Maya: "And what about that woman who for years disguised herself in blackface, and even served as the president of a NAACP chapter, and when she was discovered to be white she said she didn't lie about it because she always considered herself to be black, and therefore she had a right to be whatever she *says* she is."

Roy: "Well, there may be a second motive here. When it comes to work applications, you know, minorities have an advantage. She may have found it expedient to be in disguise."

Andy: "Okay, maybe. But I've another one you won't believe. Among the various 'trans' there is also the 'trans-able.' Which means someone who had one arm cut off because he did not feel comfortable with two. He found his true identity being one-armed."

Louise: "Come on, you made it up."

Andy: "I'm telling you the way I heard it."

Ellen: "I'm not concerned about the freaks, they can be whatever they want, one-legged, one-eyed, and one-eared. I don't care. I'm worried about the kids. Do you know that hugging or kissing in kindergarten is now banned? A five-year old boy has been accused of 'sexual harassment' for giving a female schoolmate a little peck on the cheek." She looks at Alan who has kept quiet for a while. "What d'you think about this?"

Alan: "Well, perhaps, this is a bit extreme."

Jim has listened quietly and taken in every word. Now, he has a suggestion. "Alright. You all seem to be of the same mind on this subject. And I'm with you, by the way. Let's play a game. Give me your best examples of PC insanity in ten words. Ellen, you go first."

Ellen: "The truth has become an insult. To say that Asian students are good in math is racist."

Maya: "Same thing with blacks. To say that a black is articulate is racist. It's considered a 'microaggression'."

Andy: "A short person must be referred to as 'height challenged'."

Roy: "There is no longer juvenile delinquency, it's been changed to 'justice involved youth'."

Charles: "'Illegal aliens' is an offensive term. They must be referred to as 'undocumented workers'."

Andy: "And the massacre at Fort Hood by an Islamic jihadist must be called 'work place violence.'"

Tony, coming back with Susie hand in hand: "Do not forget the most egregious of all, the Affordable Care Act, commonly known as Obamacare, which is neither affordable nor caring."

Louise: "In Congress, they 'had to pass it in order to find out what's in it' said Nanny the Speaker. None of those who tried to read it in advance could make sense of its twisted language."

Andy: "That was by design. Obama's main advisor, that prof from MIT, bragged in a video that they intentionally used deceitful language to fool the people and persuade the legislators. However, if you say that Obamacare is a fraud, just another control mechanism, you're not PC."

Charles, looking at his iPhone: "Fortunately, people are waking up. I'm looking here at some twits currently online. Listen to this…" He gets up and moves to a spot where he can be better heard by everyone. "Listen to how they define PC: 'intellectual terrorism,' 'organized hatred,' 'linguistic fascism,' 'engine of nannyism,' 'flattening of the brain,' 'worst form of censorship,' 'a social disease,' 'a straightjacket,' 'madness and maggoty,' 'the new bigotry,' 'poison to our security and defense,' and so on…"

Jim: "I'm surprised there is so much wisdom in the tweeting universe. But I welcome it. It's a heartwarming sign that the antibodies are fighting the virus."

Amy follows the discussion from a comfortable observation point, a wicker chaise nested among bushy plants whose names she doesn't know. She listens and munches on canapés offered by passing waiters, together with the finest wines from Villa Flora.

The language issue brings her back many years, to one evening in Fairville, when she had a discussion on the collapse of human civilization with her closest friends during dinner at Pete's. That evening, they came up half-jokingly with a rather pessimistic view of the future based on Foucault's warnings about the erosion of the human sciences. Their focus was on human life, receding under the assault of technology.

Nobody knew back then that most of those gloomy predictions would actually materialize in the new millennium. At first those changes were perceived as an inconvenient occurrence, then they were accepted as the 'new normal.' People are now living in a period of biological mutation. Computers govern their relationships with other people and things through series of luminous dots. Biological body parts are being routinely replaced with bionic organs and limbs. There are no robots with a human heart (yet!), but there are human beings with a robot heart. Through genetic engineering, human beings can now be generated in a petri dish, and the capacity exists to create humans by cloning, like sheep and tomatoes. Human genes are inserted into animals, animal organs into human beings. The boundaries between human being and machine, on the one hand, and between human and animal organisms, on the other, are being blurred. Human life as the principle of biology is crumbling.

The new trends are not only affecting human life but are eroding the fundamentals of society. In economics, new interfaces are being built. Labor is no longer the basis of production and wealth, the classical infrastructure that stirred a bloody class struggle a century and a half ago is gone. Now wealth is generated electronically by financial manipulation of company stocks. Conceptually, wealth has become disjointed from labor and production.

And getting back to language. Today's 'newspeak' is used mainly to obfuscate knowledge, not to acquire it. And yet, language is the very basis of knowledge, the unifying element of the human sciences, and the most distinctive feature of the human being. Because language and reason are one.

"Are you alright?" Jim asks, coming over to her. "You've been so quiet."

"I'm fine. I was thinking."

Amy looks around and realizes that the kids have left. The deck is empty.

Rosa comes looking for them. She is visibly hurried.

"Hey, guys. What're you doing here? The cake's coming

out. Come join us, and have a piece."

"Thank you. We're coming right away," Amy tells her.

Rosa rushes back.

The sun has set and the sky is getting dark. The first stars appear, still pale, still rare, against the uncertain background of the twilight.

Jim takes her by the hand and pulls her up.

"Let's take a walk on the beach. I'm sure Rosa'll put away some cake for us."

They walk down the steps and take off their shoes.

The sand is still warm. They reach the water edge and let the waves play with their feet, caressing and retreating. The ocean is deceitfully calm, its movement like a dance, its voice like an intimate murmur. The beast is asleep, ready to wake up any moment, roaring and raging against the coast, beating the rocks with frightening violence.

They do not hold hands, they walk without touching. She tells him about the thoughts she entertained a minute ago on the deck.

"What d'you think? Is this really the end of our civilization? The 9/11 attack ten years ago marked that moment of transition with dramatic symbolism. I see that episode as a watershed that divides two eras. Perhaps, future historians will refer to our time as the New Millennium, the way we talk about the Middle Ages or the Renaissance."

"9/11 was a spectacular representation of a turning point, for sure. And it'll have global implications around the world. But in our country the change started forty years ago. The cultural revolution changed society for better or for worse. The counterculture values gradually entered the mainstream and that process with time eroded our national backbone. The change came from within, and the Obama agenda is a product of it."

"D'you think we can adjust to a 'brave new world'?"

"The young will adjust and survive. You've heard them.

They have a difficult task ahead, but they seem well prepared to take on the corrosive forces poised to obliterate our system. And we… we'll fade out."

"You're fading out already. I can hardly see your face," she says jokingly.

It is dark now. The stars fill the sky, but their brightness cannot dispel the darkness. The lights on the deck are far away.

"Come close." He puts an arm around her shoulders. "I'm here, and I'm not going anywhere."

They walk back in silence, keeping pace with each other, their feet leaving symmetrical prints in the wet sand.

They reach the steps under the deck.

"Let's sit down for a minute," he says.

The party is winding down. A faint music track from the dance floor travels all the way down to the beach. It is a retro song, still emotionally powerful as when it came out fifty years ago, *So darling, darling/Stand by me, oh stand by me/Oh stand, stand by me/Stand by me.*

They sit next to each other, shoulder to shoulder, breathing in the salty breeze from the ocean.

The silhouette of the coastline is hardly visible against the dark sky. The lights on the shore mirror the stars.

Jim looks straight ahead into the darkness.

"Colleen and I are going to get a divorce."

"Oh, sorry to hear that. Did she ask for it?"

"She doesn't know yet. Tomorrow I'll break the news."

"And why, if I may ask?"

"She's not the woman for me."

Now he is looking at her, searching for her eyes.

She averts her gaze.

She cannot say what he wants to hear, that yes, they are right for each other, that she understands it now after so many years, that she'll be happy to be his wife.

And she cannot say what he does not want to hear, that

she loves her life the way it is, that she doesn't want to change it, that he's her dear, dearest friend and she loves him, but she doesn't want to be his wife.

She doesn't say anything. She listens closely to catch Stella's voice, but Stella is silent. The other stars are distant and cold. She shivers.

He pulls her close and cradles her in his arms. "You don't have to say anything. I understand."

His contagious grin comes back and lights up his eyes. "After all, we're a team." Fist bump.

CPSIA information can be obtained
at www.ICGtesting.com
Printed in the USA
BVOW00s2153211016

465692BV00001B/2/P

9 780997 496215